The Light in Dorky Walker

KILLDEER

The Light in Dorky Walker

R.E. Robb

authorHOUSE®

AuthorHouse™
1663 Liberty Drive
Bloomington, IN 47403
www.authorhouse.com
Phone: 1-800-839-8640

First published by AuthorHouse   09/28/2011

ISBN: 978-1-4670-4288-8 (sc)
ISBN: 978-1-4670-4287-1 (hc)
ISBN: 978-1-4670-4286-4 (ebk)

Library of Congress Control Number: 2011917426

Printed in the United States of America

Unless otherwise indicated, Bible quotations are taken from the New International Version of the Holy Bible. Copyright (c) 1993, 1978, 1984, 1995, by the International Bible Society.

Dedication

This story is for my grandsons; Zackary, Spencer, Ethan, Lucas, Kyle and Kory, and my granddaughters; Heather, Christine, Kathryn, and Paris Dawn, and all the young men and women who are about to face the challenges
of life in this tough world.
May God bless you all.

Books by R. E. Robb:

The Golden Scimitar
"I Learned About Boating From This . . ."
Love, Money, And Other Persuasive Words

Chapter One

And God said, "Let there be light,"
and there was light.

GENESIS 1:3

The river water felt like an icy skin. It relentlessly oozed into every pore of my body, convincing my mind that I'd never be warm again. With each step the mud pulled at my shoes, slowed my progress and strained my leg muscles until they cramped, folding me into an agonizing squat. The slow-moving current flowed around and over me, pushing me downward toward the muck of the flooded corn field.

Paralyzing fear was replaced by a pounding blackness and my unheard cries were swept away by the churning, black current.

Suddenly, it seemed that I was looking up into a high, round, silo-like room with a coil, like a spring, encircling the inside. A huge, black spider sat atop the coil and began to bounce on the spring. Little by little, the spider recoiled the spring closer and closer to me at the bottom. There was no escape. The spider became larger and larger, closer and closer, until it was within inches of my face. I screamed. The spider's hairy legs reached for me. Something hit me on the back—hard. I lay over the rough surface of what felt like a log. My ribs were about to break. I vomited and my throat burned like I'd swallowed 100 hornets.

"Easy lad. Easy! Ah, thank God, Mon, you're breathin' again and gettin' shed of that scum water you've been adrinkin'."

He was a big man in a black suit, standing in swirling brown water up to his waist. He had a puffy, red face and wheezed like an over-stoked stove. He dragged me from the log, picked me up and easily threw me over his shoulder. I threw-up again, all down the back of his suit. I seemed to be only half-awake. I could hear the water rushing, the man panting, and I could feel the movement as he carried me along, but I couldn't see anything—it was as if my eyes were glued shut. Soon the noise of the water died and I began to see foggy images of a path, trees and tall grass. I was bounced up a stairway, my head clipping the doorjamb as we entered a screened-in room. As we went through a second doorway, I dodged another head whack and he lowered me into a chair much more gently than he had thrown me over his broad shoulder.

I could make-out what looked like an old hermit's cabin I'd seen in the woods. It had rough wooden walls, planked floors, and a bunk bed in one corner. The table was hewn from a single large tree, and a braided rug on the floor was the only thing that looked to be store-bought.

He put a kettle on the stove, handed me a towel and said, "I'll have ye some hot chocolate soon, and there's some fruit, lad." He pulled off his coat, wadded it up and tossed it back into the screened porch that had only one section of screen left, the others ragged and freely flapping in the wind. The window panes rattled when he closed the door.

"Are ye feelin' okay lad?" he said in a rumbling voice. "How'd ya come by bein' in that old Mississippi floodwater?" He had an accent that I didn't recognize, and his neatly trimmed gray beard bobbed up and down as he spoke.

"I'm feelin' better now. I was sleepin' under the railroad bridge." My voice sounded raspy, and my words made my throat hurt.

"Aye, that old bridge fell apart this mornin' in the flood. You're lucky, you are, that you weren't killed when she collapsed." He poured a bit of water from a bottle over his hands, lathered them in the sink and rinsed with more of the bottled water. "Sleepin' in a place like that is not as comfortable as in a proper bed, y'know sonny, And what be your name, lad?"

I hesitated. That question always made my stomach churn, sending beads of sweat popping out all over my forehead like popcorn.

"Dorky Walker, sir."

"Wazzat? I didn't hear ya."

Louder I croaked, "My name's Walker, sir, Dorky Walker." Fearing the usual laughter and ridicule I stumbled to my feet, and prepared to head out the door and back into the flood if he made fun of my name. And I knew he would. Everyone did. Like Nate Knowles in the fourth grade who called me "Dumb Dork" and pushed me around saying I was "A really dorky jerk." He bullied everybody though, and I tried to ignore him, until one day he shoved me back down the cafeteria steps three times. I was hungry and wanted to eat, but he wouldn't let me pass. The fourth time I got mad and swung at him. I was shocked to see that I had hit him square in the left eye and sent him stumbling down the steps crying! He never bothered me again, and the other boys—and the girls too—got really friendly with me after that.

"Whadda ya want to be called, Mr. Walker?" the big man asked.

I sat back down and took a banana, dappled black with age, from a cracked glass bowl. I was starving and really cold. I didn't want to leave this food and shelter.

"You can call me Dorky." I mumbled through a mouthful. "Or just 'Dork,'" I added.

He sat two cups of hot chocolate on the table, along with knives, a plate full of toast, and some butter. "That's a wee bit of an unusual name, lad. How'd ya come by it?"

As he dropped his big frame into the rickety chair across from me, I felt pressure build up inside me, an uncontrollable swelling of emotion that I was unable to control, and I burst into tears. Ashamed and embarrassed, I skidded the chair around and tried to hide my face and my blubbering in my hands, my elbows on my knees. I was pitiful.

The man said nothing.

My sobbing stopped and I sat shuddering, ashamed of crying like a baby in front of this stranger.

"Well, I can see that you're a very unhappy young man, Mr. Dorky Walker," he said. "And if ye'd want to talk about it, I'd be pleased to heed you, lad."

I looked across the table. He was staring into his cup of hot chocolate, blowing a cooling breath onto it. I realized that I didn't know his name, who he was, or why he was helping me. This added to my embarrassment. "I'm sorry, Mr. . . ."

"MacAndrew's my name lad, Jamison MacAndrew." Most call me Mac, or Jamie," he said. "I prefer 'Mac' though." He took a sip of his cocoa.

"Now that you know who I am, Mr. Dorky Walker, might you not be willing to answer my question about your name? Who gave it to you lad?"

"Unkie, my mother's brother, told me that Momma named me, but she didn't write too good and wrote 'Dorkey' instead of the name she wanted for me, 'Darcy.' On the hospital paper her 'A' looked like an 'O' and her 'C' looked like a 'K', so it came out Dorky instead of Darcy. I didn't ever know my father. Unkie was momma's brother, and his last name was Walker, same as momma's So, at the hospital I was named Dorky Walker."

"Where's ye 'Unkie' now, boy?" he asked.

"Momma went to heaven when I was little and Unkie kept me until he went, too," I felt like I was going to cry again and bit down on my lip until it hurt. "I found him dead one mornin'. He was in the kitchen. Some people took him away and I guess they didn't know I was there. I stayed until the food was all gone and nobody came around any more looking for Unkie or me."

#

I remembered that awful morning when I went into the kitchen and found Unkie face-down on the linoleum, coffee splattered all over the floor and one wall. He wasn't breathing and his eyes were staring at the oven like he was waiting for some muffins to get done baking. His favorite coffee cup was shattered, its pieces scattered among the puddles on the floor. He was the closest thing I ever had to a father, and I pushed and pounded on his chest and cried at him not to do this. But he was gone. I finally gave up and swung the back door open so his friend, Walter, could come right in. Walter picked him up every morning and gave him a ride to work. Unkie didn't even have a car, nor much else. Now he didn't even have his life. Walter would find him and know what to do. I swore right then that I'd not be like Momma and Unkie. I would work hard and some day I would be somebody, and have all the things they only saw other people enjoy.

I went back up to my bedroom and cried into my pillow until I heard Walter's agonized moan when he found Unkie. I hid.

#

Mac sat back in his chair, his fingers laced together across his ample belly, and said nothing.

"I guess I ought to be goin," I said as I started to get up to leave.

"Nay laddie!" he roared. "You'll not be goin' back out there to be drowned or lost to the evil of this world!" He pointed to the bunk bed.

"You'll be takin' the top bunk, and I'll have the lower one, and perhaps we'll both get a much-needed night's sleep." He rose and pulled the covers back on the top space.

"You'll nae more be asleepin' under rickety bridges, laddie!"

He tossed me a clean, dry shirt that was large enough to be a nightgown, and told me to wash-up as best I could at the sink. "Be spare with the water though, lad, 'tis all we have!" He warned me, and went into the bathroom. I stood looking around the room, scared of this stranger, yet unwilling to race out the door into the cold loneliness of the night. Besides, it had been nearly three weeks since I slept in a real bed. Tonight there'd be no hard rocky place with bugs crawling on me and drunken men stumbling over me and cursing. It wouldn't be freezing cold, and, in the morning, there would be food that I wouldn't have to scrounge for in other people's trash.

I stayed.

I washed my face and hands and took a swipe at my armpits and pulled the big shirt over me. It hung almost to the floor and the neck hole was so big that it could slip clean over my shoulders. Just then Mr. MacAndrew came out of the bathroom.

"Ah, me lad, you're ready for the bed, are ye?"

I nodded.

"And sure that's good, but before you sleep, we must talk to Our Father and thank him for bringin' you out of the valley and unto the still waters."

I didn't know what he was talking about, so I just nodded and stood there hoping he'd tell me what he meant.

"We'll pray now lad," he said. "Did your Momma pray with you, or your . . . what did you call him . . . *Unksomething* . . . know God?"

"No, sir." I'd heard of praying and that some folks believed in God and sometimes they kind of went crazy with jumping around and screaming and such. I hoped Mr. MacAndrew wasn't going to do nothing crazy.

"That be the case, we'll be a-kneelin' by the bed here." He went down on one knee and motioned me to do the same at the other end of the bed.

"Our dear Heavenly Father, this auld man and this wee boy come to you this night with great thanks for bringin' us together in this house. You've surely provided so many blessin's and have given so much to us to be thankful for, we praise ye, Lord,"

I thought he was finished, and I started to stand up, then he went on.

"We ask that ye keep and protect those periled by the floods and continue to watch over all of us. We send this prayer in Jesus' holy name, Amen."

I just got kneeled, and he finished, and I bounced up again.

"We need to be constantly thankful for all our blessin's and tell God that we are. Always remember that, lad," He sat on the bottom bed and pointed to a narrow, rickety-lookin' ladder at the end of the bunk bed.

"Up you go, and sleep well."

The flimsy ladder creaked and I banged my knee trying to swing into the bed.

"You alright?" he called.

"Yes, sir. Thank you." I plopped down and felt the springs poking up through the thin mattress. But when I lay down and pulled the sheet and cover over me, it was soft and warm, better than any bed I could ever remember—and there was a pillow! I heard a soft snore from Mr. MacAndrew and I fell into a deep, restful sleep.

Noises woke me up, and I snuggled deeply into the covers and pillow, laying quietly and listening to Mr. MacAndrew at work in the kitchen.

The smell of coffee, the sizzling of bacon and the sound of eggs being cracked into a pan. I rolled over, faced the room and smelled the cooking.

"Aaahhh, there he is!" Mac said. "Alive and well, and I'd bet a bit hungry too, what?"

"Yes, I'm always hungry," I croaked. My throat was still raw from vomiting the night before.

"Well, jump on down here, get dressed, and we'll have a bite before we take on the day, whadda ye say?"

By the time I came out of the bathroom, there were two plates with eggs, bacon and some white lumpy things, cups of coffee and two small glasses of orange juice. It was the most breakfast I'd ever seen. Momma usually fixed a bowl of oatmeal and a half glass of milk—never anything like this. Unkie just made toast. He taught me to like coffee, even though he said I was too young to be drinking it.

I pulled myself up to the table and took the fork to the eggs.

"No lad!" Mac stopped my hand on its way to my opened mouth.

"What's wrong?"

"Do you like the likes of this breakfast, lad?" he calmly asked.

"Sure! It's about the best I've ever seen!" I exclaimed.

"Well now. How and where do ya think we came by this here meal?"

I sat silently, unable to come up with an answer, my mouth still hanging open.

"All things, everythin' that we have—our food, our clothin', our shelter—is provided by God." He pointed up toward the ceiling. I automatically looked up, then felt foolish.

"Aye lad, we'll thank our Lord for our food before every meal and before we take a bite, like this, alright?"

I nodded and put my hands in my lap and bowed my head as he did.

He began, "Forgive us Father, our dear Lord, for our eagerness to get into this meal. We've not had much to eat, y'know, but we are eternally grateful for this food, and for all the marvelous blessin's that we enjoy as Your children . . ."

"Pffft!" I was unable to stop the laughter, and it spewed out like the steam from Momma's old tea kettle.

"What do ye find so funny, boy?" He didn't look angry, just sort of surprised.

"I'm sorry, sir," I was grinning. "But you said we are 'children!'"

"Aye, laddie, we are all children of God. Do you know nothin' of the Bible?"

"Yes . . . I mean, no." He had a way of making questions hard to answer. "I mean, I know that there is a Bible, but I don't know what's in it or why folks read it."

He continued his prayer as if I never interrupted it, ". . .and ask that You continue to bless us as family in Your house. Amen. We can eat now," he said softly.

I left my head bowed and my hands in my lap for a few moments. I guess he thought I went to sleep, "lad, ye can eat now," he said loudly.

"I'm sorry, sir. I was just tellin' God that I'm sorry I laughed while you were sayin' your prayer."

His face lit-up and a wide smile spread almost to his ears. Big crinkly lines wrinkled-up the sides of his eyes. "That's beautiful, lad," he said as he raised his hands as if they were playing an accordion, "You've said your first prayer! Glory be to God!"

We finished the breakfast in conversation and with a lot of laughter. He seemed to be happy that I'd prayed, and I felt good.

While Mac washed the plates, I looked out the door and saw the muddy water that had broken through the levee during the last storm. It was not as high, and wasn't rushing by as fast as the day before. Way off in the distance I could see only the roofs of some houses above the swirling brown water. Two men in a boat rowed along where the street should have been. Mac's house was well above the water level and dry. But, when we left, we still had to wade through knee-deep water that was only a little ways from the house.

"Where are we goin'?" I was nervous being back into the heavy, dirty water and I stayed close to the big man lest I be dragged under again.

"We're going to Kirkcaldy Christian Church. We've work to do today. That is, unless you have other plans."

Chapter Two

You, LORD, are my lamp; the LORD
turns my darkness into light.

2 SAMUEL 22:29

Kirkcaldy Christian Church stood on a grassy hillside. The ancient, wooden structure leaned downhill, its foundation seemingly ready to let the sagging eaves, peeling paint, broken stairs, and warped hand rails be taken by gravity down the slope and into the swamp.

We went up the hill, slipping and sliding on the wet grass. I was getting more and more curious about this man. That had never happened to me before. I usually didn't care to know anything about anybody. I figured they was none of my business. But Mac didn't tell me anything about himself unless I asked.

"What does 'Kirkcaldy' mean?"

"Ah, that's what you people here in America call my 'home town.' It's in Scotland."

"Scotland?"

"Aye, lad." He stopped and scratched at his beard. "'Tis a grand, big country far across the ocean. Rollin' hills, all green and lush, with hundreds, nay, thousands, of 'lochs,' what you call 'lakes,' and Kirkcaldy is the 'lang toun' on the Firth of Forth in the east of Scotland. That means 'long town.' It's called that because her main street runs for miles along the waterfront on an inlet called the 'Firth of Forth.'"

He stood with his face to the sky, a slight grin pushing up one side of his mouth.

"You miss bein' there, don't you."

"Aye, 'tis hard to shake a person's home from the pockets of his mind." He continued up the hill.

We came up to the side of the church. A narrow road led to the front of the ramshackle place. "Why didn't we take the road?" I asked.

"Well, lad, just beyond those trees to the left, the road drops down and is under water. Flooded, y'know." He leaned against the railing leading up to the front door, puffing like he'd just run a mile. "And right here," he pointed to the right, "is the end of the road." He laughed a short bitter sort of a snort. "Aye, he said softly, "perhaps it's the end of the road for me as well."

Leading the way up stairs, he pushed the door open and walked slowly inside, looking from side to side and up and down. "Come along, lad."

I wondered what he was looking for inside the church, but figured he'd tell me if he wanted. I walked in a few steps behind him, looking around like he did, and seeing nothing but dust-covered benches, some Bibles, and ragged song books scattered among the seats.

As if he could hear my thoughts, he said, "Have to be watchful for animals that take refuge here when I'm away." He reached down and brought up a writhing snake a couple of feet long. "Like this bonny lassy here. She's a reg'lar in my church. Sure and more reg'lar than any of the local folks." He went to the door and gently placed the snake outside.

I looked around a room that was only big enough for a handful of people. There were four rows of benches on each side of the aisle with room for about six people on each bench. In the front there was a raised platform with a small table and an old upright piano wedged into the corner. The walls were white, but unlike the outside, the paint was not peeling and flaking.

"Now lad," he said, "time for you to earn your keep. Would you be openin' the curtains on all the windows please, and be gentle with them as they are a bit delicate with age." Again the snort-like laugh.

I went right to it. The curtains once had been white, but were now a dusty gray, torn and stained.

"And ye'll find a box of rags under the back pew. Please to be wipin' the dust and dirt offen the seats, would you now."

Sometimes Mac was hard to understand. I guess it was from being from another country.

We worked for an hour or so, but the place didn't look much better.

"We'll be ready now for the first service," he said, and sat down on the piano bench, reading his Bible and making notes on a small pad. "You just rest easy now, boy, and let me study here for a bit."

I lay down on a bench and stared up at the ceiling. There was no ceiling actually, just rafters and then the underside of the roof. Brown stains showed where the leaks were.

I thought that no one had ever treated me as an equal, or left me alone to do things on my own, even if it was only wiping off seats and opening curtains. I began to wonder how it would be if he was my father. It was a feeling I'd never had before.

Startled awake by a bell ringing loudly, I jumped up and Mac was not there. I ran to the front door and there he was, standing on the porch, ringing a bell with one hand, his Bible tucked under his other arm. He gave me a smile and said, "Good mornin' to ye, young Dorky Walker, welcome to Kirkcaldy Christian Church!"

I stood just inside the doorway until he finished. "What are you doin'?" I asked.

"Ah, lad, I'm summonin' the faithful to worship. Now take a seat up front and we'll soon start the service."

I sat all the way against the wall on the front bench and waited. Smiling, Mac walked down the aisle, and stepped up behind a funny little table with a slanted top. He carefully sat the Bible down, and stood silently looking at it. "Let us pray," he said softly.

Suddenly his deep voice echoed throughout the small church, rising and falling like thunder on a stormy night. He stood, eyes closed, his head and arms raised upward, and his body vibrating with each word.

He finished with a gentle "Amen."

His eyes scanned the empty seats as he told the story of Jesus and how he raised Lazarus from his death bed. Sometimes smiling, sometimes angry, he echoed throughout the empty room. I sneaked a look behind me and saw that he and I were still the only ones in the church. His preaching went on for a long time until he finally paused, looked at me and said, "Let us pray."

He finished the prayer, leaned over the little table and softly asked me, "Do ye perhaps play the piano, lad?" I shook my head, and he smiled and said some words about a hymn and began to sing. His voice boomed through the building, rattling windows and causing a small bird to fly from the rafters and out the door. I listened to the words of a song I'd never heard before, and wanted to sing with him, but couldn't.

He finished and picked-up his Bible. The little church was still vibrating as we left.

We walked silently for a while, then he said, "Thank you for helping me this day." I nodded and we continued on to his house where he fixed us sandwiches and glasses of milk.

"Why so quiet, boy?" he asked.

"I was thinkin' of the song. I guess I would have liked to sing with you like I've seen done before."

"And where would that be, lad?"

I told him that Unkie took me to a German place called a beer garden and all the people swung their glasses around and sang songs. Then they'd drink some, then sing some more.

He laughed and said that it must have been a German Oktoberfest celebration.

I didn't know what it was, but I remembered that it was fun.

"Can you read?" he asked.

"Pretty good," I allowed.

"Aye, then. We'll be back to the church for the evenin' service and what you do, you see, is take up one of those books on the bench, not the Bible, the other one. It's a hymnal. I'll tell you which number it is in the book that we'll be singin', and you just go to that page and sing along."

"I can do that for the words, but how about the tune?"

"Ah, just listen to the first go-around, then you'll know the tune and you can sing along when it repeats. How's that?"

We hiked into town to buy some more food. I told him some more of how I came to be alone, and he told me some more of how he came to be alone too.

The town was Quickville and looked about as long as a corn field, with only a main street and smaller streets on the sides lined with old houses and a couple of warehouse-like buildings. It was above the river and wasn't flooded, but it also had a pier along the riverbank that was nearly under water. A small market was the largest of the shops along the short street that was "town." It was a wooden building, and the floor creaked under us as though we would fall through if we didn't walk softly. It was smoky inside from four men sitting around a small table playing cards. A pair of crutches leaned against the table near one man. They looked embarrassed when Mac came in, and they put the cards under a newspaper. I remembered how I would choke from the cigarette smoke when I went into Mama's room. I didn't like it much. I went back outside and petted a big sad-eyed dog that was curled up on the sidewalk.

I was leaning on the back of a chair out on the wooden sidewalk when a man came around the corner. Tall and skinny, he wore a suit and tie and hat. I couldn't remember how long it had been that I'd seen a man in a suit and tie and hat. His face was long, like a horse's, and looked all wrinkly.

"Hi there, son," he said, and smiled, showing yellowed crooked teeth. "Where you belong?"

"Oh, I'm with Mr. MacAndrew," I said. "He's in the store there."

"Ah, the good Rev. Mac." He pulled a pad of paper from his coat pocket and a pencil came from someplace by his ear. "And what is your name, son?"

I didn't want to talk to him, and I didn't want to tell him my name, because like always, I feared that he'd make fun of me and loudly point out my name to anybody who'd listen. It always happened like that. I turned and went back into the smoke-filled grocery.

"Hello, Rev. Mac," he said. He had followed me into the store.

Mr. MacAndrew looked up and said hello to the man but didn't seem to be very friendly toward him. He put his hand on my shoulder and said, "Dorky, this is Mason Quick, he's the editor of our newspaper here in town, *The Quickville Courier*. Mr. Quick's family settled this area back in the '20s and the town's named after his great, great, grandfather, Madison Quick.

"Good to meetcha," I muttered.

Mac took Mr. Quick's arm and walked him toward the door, speaking softly and urgently to the man. He returned and said, "OK, Dorky, you can talk to Mr. Quick. He'll not ask about your name."

I was grateful to Mac and took no time to get back outside, away from the choking smoke.

Mr. Quick smiled at me as he came out the door and said, "The Good Rev. told me your name. Interesting." He poised the pencil on the pad. "How'd you meet him and where you from?"

I told him the story of Mama and Unkie, and the bridge falling down, and me almost drowning, and Mr. MacAndrew pulling me out of the water, going to his church and then to this store. I was almost out of breath when I finished.

Mr. Quick had been writing frantically and asked me lots of questions, nodding and sometimes sticking the end of the pencil on his tongue. I didn't understand that, and hoped to remember to ask Mac why he does that.

Before he could ask another question, I said. "Why do you call Mr. MacAndrew that name, you know, 'Revern?'"

He laughed, "No, it's '*Reverend*.' That's what we call preachers around here." He went back to his note-taking.

I heard Mac call to me from inside the store. "Aye, Dorky, will you give me a bit of a hand here!" I rushed in.

One of the men at the table slid his chair back and gave a mule-like laugh. "Dorky! Did you call that boy 'Dorky?'"

The other men smiled or outright laughed. Mac stepped to the edge of the table and lifted the first man out of his chair by the collar of his shirt. The other man's crutches fell to the floor.

"You'll nae be makin' fun 'o me friend here, Johnny." His voice was low and menacing. The man's eyes grew round and big. Mac went on, "His name is Dorky Walker, and you can call him 'Mr. Walker,' or

'Dorky,' or 'lad,' or 'son,' but whatever you call him, do it with respect, *Johnny Small Head.*"

The man nodded and said, "Sorry, Mac. No offense intended there." Mac lowered the man back into the chair and straightened the collar where he'd grabbed onto him. He replaced the fallen crutches. "We'll be seein' ye all *next* Sunday, I hope. God be with you, lads."

Mac loaded me up with an armful of bags of groceries. He picked up the rest, smiled at the men, said, "Good day," and we left the store.

Mr. Quick was gone, and I asked Mac, "Why did you call that man *Small Head?*"

"Well, lad, because that's his name." he smiled. "He was born of an Indian family out in the swamp. Came here as a wee babe when his parents became ill and passed on. The townsfolk took him in, fed and kept him well, and schooled him and now he's in charge of the town dump and the Sanitation Department. But as for your question; the Indians gave him the name 'Small Head' and we just gave him the name 'Johnny.'"

Chapter Three

In him was life, and that light was the light of men. The light shines in the darkness, but the darkness has not understood it.

JOHN 1:5

After putting away the groceries, Mac and I returned to the church. It was starting to get dark as we went into the building, Mac checking for critters. We lit candles at the front and back of the room. I picked-up one of the song books and began to look through it, the flickering candlelight was just enough light so that I could see the words.

Again, Mac went outside and rang the church bell. Ding-dong, ding-dong, ding-dong, seven times. he walked, smiling, down the aisle, glancing left and right as if looking for people to be in the seats. There was not one soul there except me.

Mac smiled at me, took his place behind the little slanted-top table and again said, "Let us pray."

As his opening prayer ended, I heard a scuffling behind me. I twisted around and saw an old woman and a skinny, red-headed boy about my age,12 or 13 I guessed. They moved slowly down the aisle and took seats in the second row, ignoring me and watching Mac, eager to hear his sermon.

Mac pretty much repeated the sermon he said that morning and I learned some things from it that I had missed before. This led me to believe that hearing something over and over will make you remember it better. I wanted to remember to ask Mac about that later. When he had finished his talk, we sang Hymn No. 22. After I heard the tune, I was able to join Mac in singing the rest. Mac's big voice made me able to sing my loudest without being heard too much. The woman and boy sat silently and looked at the floor while we sang.

The service over, Mac went to the door and waited as the woman and boy moved down the aisle to leave. He hugged the lady and shook the young man's hand, smiling and nodding at them. "Hey there laddie," he called out to me. "Be comin' here, would ye please!"

When Mac told me the boy's name was Willie, the boy said, "Whadda ya say?" It wasn't a question, more like just a greeting. "Hi. Not much," I muttered, again nervous about meeting him because I knew he'd make fun of my name. People always did. Mac and the lady were talking and Willie said, "So, your name's Dorky, right?" He wasn't grinning or sneering at me.

"Yeah, Dorky Walker," I said.

"Cool. My name's Willie Gilley."

"Cool," I said.

"Yeah, I'm goin' to call you 'Dor' and you can call me 'Wil,' okay?"

"Sure will, Wil." We both laughed at my "will Wil."

"Ain't nobody gonna make fun of our names, right?"

"Right, Wil."

For the first time that I could ever remember I had a friend with a funny name too.

On the walk back to the house, Mac told me that Wil's daddy had been caught trying to steal a truck and beat-up the farmer. He ran away, and hadn't been heard of for almost a year. Mac had been able to help them with some money, but since the flood, no money had come in, and he could only give Wil's momma a few dollars.

"Why didn't they want to sing with you?"

"Oh, lad," he said. "I think that they may have wanted to sing with us, but y'see, Mrs. Gilley and her boy cannot read the words in the hymnal."

That night we had a small dinner and prayed for the Gilleys.

After dinner I asked Mac, "Does God hear everybody's prayin'?"

Yes, it is in the Bible, he said, that God hears everyone's prayers.

"Even mine?"

"Yes, even yours. And if you ask God to come into your life and you repent of all of your sins and sinful ways, God will send His Holy Spirit to live inside you to lead and direct you."

"I don't know what my sins are."

Mac laughed. "My boy, I doubt that you have any sins of any consequence. But be sure, lad, sinnin' will come upon you as The Devil finds out that you are acceptin' God and His son, Jesus Christ."

"How do I do that?" I had a strange feeling that it was important that I ask God into my life, like Mac said.

"Well, my young Mr. Walker," said Mac, "just repeat after me, slowly, and listen to every word. As we say it, be sure that ye mean it, okay?" He put his hand on my head. "Close your eyes, think about what we're sayin' right?"

"Yessir."

He began, "Our dear heavenly Father, this boy comes to You this night with a desire that You come into his life."

I repeated his words before I forgot what he said.

"He gives his life to You. We ask that his name be written in the Lamb's Book O'Life. We ask this in the name of Your Holy son, Jesus, who went to the cross and died for us, so that our sins might be washed away. Thank you Lord. Amen."

I was able to repeat everything, and asked if it was okay for me to say that prayer again.

"Oh, and to be sure, laddie. You can pray anytime, as much as you like. It'll bring you peace, it will," he said.

"Will God help me to be like you, and Mr. Quick—y'know, an important person?"

Mac said that it was important that I read the Bible and learn as much as I could from it, and everything would come to me. It would take work, he said, but he knew that I could do it. I was pretty good at reading, and eager to try. I wanted to learn more. Someday, I would be more successful than Momma and Unkie.

Before we went to bed, Mac read from the Bible, explaining things that I didn't understand. He was the best teacher I ever had. That night he read from the Gospel of John.

"In the beginning was the Word, and the Word was with God, and the Word was God. He was with God in the beginning."

"Who was?" I asked.

"Jesus. He was God, and came to earth as a man." said Mac. He continued, *"Through him all things were made that has been made. In him was life, and that light was the light of men. The light shines in the darkness, but the darkness has not understood it."* He closed the Bible and rubbed his eyes.

"You see, lad, Jesus is the light of men. The light of the world. And that brings us hope." He got up and carried the plates to the sink. "God said, *'Let light shine out of the darkness.'* And he made his light to shine in our hearts."

I washed as best I could in the little bowl and used just a little from the bottle of water. I undressed and put on the big shirt just as Mac pushed the bathroom door open. I headed for the top bunk bed.

"Pastor Mac," I said, "thanks for putting God in me!"

"I didn't do it, my dear friend," he said softly, "you did it. Now go to sleep."

I scrunched down under the cold covers. *"Let light shine out of the darkness. And he made his light to shine in our hearts."* I remembered what Mac said, and I repeated the prayer asking for God to come into my life. I think I got it pretty right. I was lying on my back with the covers tucked tightly under my chin and thinking about how much I'd learned in these few days being here with Mac. His rumbling snore began.

My eyes were closed and I had only blackness to see. Then I thought I saw a small spot of light in the center of the blackness. *"Let light shine out of the darkness. And he made his light to shine in our hearts."*

"Is that you, God?" I said aloud, but softly.

The light went out, then came back on, still small, a bright pinpoint in the blackness.

"God, did you hear my prayin'?" Again my light blinked off, then on.

"God, is your Holy . . . umm, y'know, what Mac said would come into me?" The light blinked off, and I felt, I guess it just came to me, like I just suddenly kind of knew what I was trying to remember. *"Holy Spirit!* That's it!" And my light returned.

A feeling of peace came on me and in spite of my excitement, I slept.

\#

In Quickville, Mason Quick pulled a copy of the *Quickville Courier* from the stack of newspapers being trimmed at the end of his small printing press. He scanned the pages, then settled down in his squeaky office chair to read what he had written for the lead story. It took-up most of the front page and read:

Quickville, November 12, 1956. A young man's life was snatched from certain death in the floodwaters of North County Saturday by local preacher, Jamison MacAndrew, pastor of the Kirkcaldy Christian Church in Quickville.

The vagrant boy, who wished his name withheld, was pulled unconscious from John Dolbie's cornfield just as Rev. MacAndrew saw him disappear under the rushing water, caused by a breach in the North County levee.

"I saw him struggling to stay afoot, then he was suddenly sucked under by the force of the water's flow," said MacAndrew. "I simply reached him and pulled him out in time."

MacAndrew carried the boy to his home and is assisting in the recovery of his health. The boy is homeless and spent the previous night under the North Fork railroad bridge, narrowly averting death there as well, when the bridge collapsed early Saturday morning.

The story went on to give more details of the flood and Rev. MacAndrew's history in Quickville, and finished with:

Pastor MacAndrew is to be commended for his unselfish dedication to the North County area, Quickville, and to the rescue of this unfortunate young man.

A short story of county workers dumping truckloads of rock into the space eroded in the levee accompanied the MacAndrew story. There were two photos sharing the page; one of the broken levee with the water rushing through the gap, and an old one of Jamison MacAndrew.

Mason Quick placed the paper on the desk, satisfied with his work. In this rural area, there was precious little news to report, and he was thankful for the MacAndrew story. Perhaps it will stimulate some advertising business, he thought.

Mason Quick gathered up sheets of labels for this subscriber mailing, and went to work preparing the Friday morning distribution of the *Courier*.

#

Me and Pastor Mac, as I began to call him, had Bible study after dinner every night, except Saturday, when he needed to prepare his sermon for the next day's service. He sometimes took notes during our Bible studies, when he read something he wanted to use in his sermon. Sometimes I asked a question or make a suggestion that made Pastor Mac excited, and he'd write notes like crazy. He always told me that I was a gift from God whenever that happened. I didn't think that I was a gift from God—I thought he was.

Sometimes he would read a Bible verse that made me think of the light I was seeing. Up to that point I never told Pastor Mac about my light, thinking that he'd think I was crazy. One night he read 2 PETER 1:19: *"And we have the word of the prophets made more certain, and you will do well to pay attention to it, as to a light shining in a dark place, until the day dawns and the morning star rises in your hearts."*

It said that I should pay attention to the light in a dark place. I knew then that I had to always pay attention to my light and respect it. Because it really was God. I wanted to talk about this with Pastor Mac, but it had to be a perfect time, and I had to be sure my light would still be there for me. I began to think of my light as a person, God, inside of me. And I guess that's what it was.

The week went by fast. Pastor Mac was worried about money. It made me worry, so one night I closed my eyes and waited for my light. I said, "Dear God, are you there for me?" Then it was there. Just a small dot of light right in the center of the blackness of my closed eyes. "God," I said. "Pastor Mac is worried and I need to know what I can do to help him. I'm eatin' the food and drinkin' the coffee, and I should be helpin' to pay for that stuff. Whadda ya' say?"

The light went off, then back on. "Okay, Father, what can I do? Get a job maybe?" No answer. "I don't have anythin' to sell." No blink of my light. "Okay, I get it. You just want me to trust you, right?" The light blinked at me.

Pastor Mac and I went to Quickville that Friday and saw Mr. Quick hurrying down the street, his arms full of *Quickville Couriers*. He waved at us, and hurried over.

"Ah, Rev. MacAndrew and his young charge," he said. "I was hoping I would see you this morning."

He handed Pastor Mac one of the newspapers and turned to me.

"Son, I need some help today getting the newspaper out to my subscribers. Can you read names and addresses and such?"

I told him that I surely could.

"I'd be paying you one . . ." He stopped and looked at Pastor Mac looking at him. "Yes, well, I'll pay you *two* dollars an hour to take these newspapers to the addresses on them. Think you can do that?"

I said that I surely could, and load me up with them!

I spent the rest of the day running from house to house and back to Mr. Quick's office for more newspapers. It wasn't hard work, and the people I met were nice and friendly, and I only got chased by a dog once. Its owner whistled real loud just before the dog got to me.

The sun was dipping down behind the low hills to the west when I finally finished. I was tired and hungry.

Mr. Quick was in his office and I told him I'd finished the job. He gave me eight dollars cash! I'd never had that much money at one time, and I ran to the grocery store to tell Mac. He was talking with the store's owner and I waited until they were finished, hopping from one foot to the other with excitement.

Finally, "Pastor Mac, look!" I shouted. He smiled, took the eight dollars, counted it and said, "Let us go and see Mr. Quick, shall we, lad?"

I didn't know why, but I said okay.

Mr. Quick was still in his office and Mac walked right in and right up to his desk.

"Mason," he said with a deep rumble to his voice. "I understand you offered the lad two dollars for each hour he worked. Am I correct?"

Mr. Quick said, "That's right Rev. Is there a problem?"

"Well, I don't think there's a problem. If there is, we can straighten it out, can't we."

"Of course." said Mr. Quick.

"Ah, well then," Pastor Mac continued. "I reckon the boy started right away today at about noon, didn't he."

"Yes." Mr. Quick looked a little pale and ran a finger around inside his shirt collar.

"And it looks like he finished just a bit ago at about 6p.m., isn't that so?"

"Oh my goodness!" said Mr. Quick. "You're right. That's *six* hours not four! How could I have made such a mistake?" He pulled four more dollars from his pocket and handed them to Pastor Mac.

"It's the boy's. Give it to him."

I took the bills and was almost shaking with excitement at having so much money.

"And thank ye for the story, Mason. You did a fine job of telling the facts." He took my arm and steered me out the door.

On the way home, I handed the four dollars to Pastor Mac. He poked it into his shirt pocket without a word.

At his house, Pastor Mac began to make our dinner, and I fell asleep with my head on the kitchen table. I was tired from all the running around I did that day.

I woke up to the sweet smell of pork chops and beans. Mac came to the table and we said grace and then he put the 12 dollars next to my plate. "Here ye are, lad. Keep it in a safe place, don't y'know."

"No Mac!" I said too loud. "That's for the food and everythin' that you've been payin' for. I got no use for it. My light said I would be gettin' it."

I immediately was sorry I blurted-out that about 'my light'—I wasn't ready yet to talk about it, but I guessed that I'd have to now.

He silently tasted his beans. "Do ye know about 'tithing' lad?"

I said that I didn't know what that was or even how to say it.

"God's people, that's you and me, give the first 10 percent of their money, assets, whatever of value, to God, through the church."

He munched on a pork chop, then went on, "So if you are a good Christian boy, you should give 10 percent of your 12 dollars to the church. That'd be one dollar, twenty cents. Whadda ye think of that?"

I thought about that, then said, "Okay, it'll be one dollar and twenty cents. And I owe for last week and the week before that, so that's ummm . . ."

"Three dollars, sixty cents," he volunteered.

"Can I give more, or is that wrong?"

"You can give whatever you want to, but you must give it willingly, happily, joyously. Y'see you're just giving back to God a bit of all that he's been giving to you. And you'll surely be blessed."

We finished eating and he said, "What about this 'light' you spoke of?"

I explained how I had begun to see the small bright light at night when my eyes were closed, and how it answered my questions by blinking off and then on again. I told him that my light was God in me, and that I can talk to my light and get answers, and today it made me able to get some money for us by delivering the newspapers, "Just like it promised last night."

Mac took off his glasses, rubbed his eyes and said, "Praise be to God, lad. You are truly blessed."

Chapter Four

As for God, his way is perfect:
The LORD's word is flawless;
he shields all who take refuge in him.

2 SAMUEL 22:31

With the hole in the levee plugged-up, the flood water had drained-off leaving a thick layer of mud behind. County crews were scraping it from the roads with what looked like a snow plow, a gang of men shoveling what was left off to the sides, into the fields. Pastor Mac thought that someday the mud would dry-up and make rich topsoil for planting. I just thought it smelled bad.

On Sunday morning we got up and got ready to go to church. I was more helpful now, making coffee and starting breakfast, Pastor Mac, dressed in his suit and tie, studied his sermon notes.

I had new pants and shirt and a pair of real leather shoes for Sunday. I washed under my arms and combed my hair too. We were using the money I earned for some things we needed, like food, bottled water and clothes. On Friday, Pastor Mac bought me an ice cream cone at the grocery store. Life was good.

We walked up the hill to the church. It was easier because the grass had dried out some. As we came up to where we could see the church, Pastor Mac stopped and said "Glory be to God!" I thought of Unkie and how he'd say things when he was surprised, but they weren't very nice like 'Glory be to God.'

A bus, two cars, and a horse-drawn wagon with mud-caked wheels and brown splatters up their sides were parked in front of the church. A lot of people were standing around talking and waving their Bibles.

We hurried up.

The people came to Pastor Mac, smiling and shaking his hand and patting his arms and back. They smiled and said that they were proud of him for what he'd done.

I whispered to him, "What'd you do?"

I have nae the foggiest idea, lad. Must be the Lord's work afoot!"

Then a group of men noticed me and said, "Rev., is this the boy whose life you saved?"

Pastor Mac looked embarrassed, "Well, I found him a-swimmin' in the corn field yon, and dried him out a bit." The men laughed and slapped him on the back as he went to open the church.

Any animals inside would have run for their lives as the crowd of townsfolk rumbled into the church, shaking the whole building like an earthquake.

Pastor Mac didn't need to ring the bell to "summon the faithful." They were all there, every seat was filled, folks jammed-in together, happily talking. Men were lined up, standing shoulder to shoulder along the side and back walls and part way out the door. I opened the curtains and was startled by faces peering in from outside. I opened the few sliding windows so they could hear the sermon. A really big lady sat down at the piano and I heard the old wooden seat creak from her weight as she began to play a beautiful song and the crowd of folks quieted down to a few coughs and sneezes and shuffling of feet.

Pastor Mac went to the pulpit (he had corrected me that it was not a "little table," but a "pulpit.") and when the music stopped, he said, "Let us pray."

He began his sermon and his eyes shone with happy pride and love for the people who had come that day.

As the last song was played and the people stood singing, he came to me and gave me a round baking pan sort of thing and said, "Would you please stand at the back door with this so that people can give their offerin' as they leave." I went back to the door and the men smiled at me, slapped me on the back, and patted me on the head. I felt like I was someone important for the first time ever.

The music ended and the people began to leave. Each of the men, and some of the women, put money in the pan I held. Everyone was smiling at me and nodding. Pretty soon the pan was about full and the last folks were talking to Pastor Mac, so I went to the front and sat down to wait for him.

"Hey Dor, what's happenin', man?" I looked up and there was Wil, smiling at me and holding out his hand. I shook his hand. That was the first time I ever shook another kid's hand. It was weird—suddenly it was like I was a grown-up. He sat next to me and we talked about things. He told me everything that he'd done in the past week and some things about the town and the people. He knew a lot.

"Our neighbor read the story in the paper to us, man," he said. "That must have been pretty scary, huh?"

I told him that I wasn't so much scared as I was confused—all mixed-up.

"Well, Rev. MacAndrew is a big hero in town now."

Now I understood what had happened. I thought all those folk were at church because the road had been cleared of mud, not because of Mr. Quick's newspaper story about Mac pulling me up out of the water.

"You're a hero too, Dor. Folks say that Rev. MacAndrew was about to leave Quickville until this happened, and nobody wanted him to go away." He punched me on the leg, "You came along just in time, pal!"

I saw Pastor Mac leave a small group. He went to where Wil's mom, Mrs. Gilley, sat. He sat down next to her and they talked for a few minutes. Seeing me watching, Mac waved me over. Wil and I went to the bench in front of them and sat backward on it.

"May I have the collection, lad." I didn't know what he meant at first. Then Wil poked me and pointed to the pan with the money in it.

Mac took out some wrinkled bills and pressed them into Mrs. Gilley's hand. She had a small, sad smile for him and wiped her eyes as if she'd been crying, or was going to. She stood, and Mac moved out of the way so that they could leave.

"See ya later, Dor," said Wil.

Mac stood silently watching them go. He seemed to be sad about something.

Outside, the people were slowly leaving in small groups and some were getting on the bus. Pastor Mac went from group to group, person to person, thanking them for coming and saying, "God bless ye!" to them all.

With everyone gone, we closed the windows and curtains, sort of cleaned up the church, arranging the Bibles and song books. Mac counted and folded the money, putting it and the coins in a small cloth bag.

We walked down the hill to the old house. Mac went to the bed, knelt, and silently prayed. I put my head down on the table and started to pray, but fell asleep.

That night Mac was quiet. I asked him if he was sad. He said that no, he was very happy, but he was thinking of the church and how we were going to need one with more room now that it looked like folks were going to be coming on Sundays. He said that he was also thinking of Mrs. Gilley. He wished he could help her more. He thanked me for my helping him that day, and said that he was "Truly blessed to have me in his life."

The moon was bright as I lay in my bed. I could see the whole inside of the small cabin, the grassy slope out the window, and a bit of the roof of the church standing just over the hill. I thought about the church, the day's event, and Wil and Mrs. Gilley. I closed my eyes thinking that the moonlight would go through my eyelids making it too bright inside to see my light. But I was wrong. After a minute or so, my light was there, small and bright.

"Our Heavenly Father," I prayed, "Thank you for bringin' all them folks to Pastor Mac's church today, and thank you for the money too. We'll do right with it, I promise." I thought for a minute, then said, "Y'know, Pastor Mac read today in the Bible that you said, *'You have not, because you ask not.'* Is that true? I mean, I know you don't lie. I think it's true because you've done all the things that I've asked. Is it true?" The light went off then came back on, just as before. It was true.

Pastor Mac told me that I should pray just as if I was talking to my Father, because I was. So I said, "Look God, Mac is worried about somethin'. I know part of it is because his church is too small, but I think it's somethin' to do with Mrs. Gilley too. I don't know what to do, but I figure that it would be best to talk to you about it." The light stayed on. "Whadda ya think, God. Can we get Mac a bigger, better church?" The light blinked off then back on. And just as suddenly, I was asleep.

On Monday morning a heavy rain beat down on us. Pastor Mac said we would stay in, taking care of housecleaning and studying the Bible. Leaks in the roof soon began to send rivulets of water cascading from a half-dozen places. Mac placed pots and pans to catch the water that we'd save for washing and flushing the toilet. The tinkling noise multiplied with each new pan, and soon it was an anvil chorus of dripping and splashing water. We kept busy emptying them. It was good that no more leaks started, because we ran out of pans. During the night, whoever happened to wake up emptied the pans into four big buckets in the bathroom, but then the noise of the water hitting the bottom of the empty pans would make it hard to go back to sleep until it became a quieter splash.

The next morning I carefully climbed down the bunk bed ladder to go to the bathroom and waded through water all the way there. Neither of us woke up during the night. The pans filled and ran over, and in the morning the entire floor of the house was one big puddle.

The rain continued most of the week, and Pastor Mac said that he feared the levee would break again, perhaps with a bigger flood than before.

On Friday the rain stopped, and after we mopped the house we went to the church to see what the damage was. The levees had held, but the walk up the hill was slippery and we both fell to our knees several times, Mac saying that God was doing it to make us kneel and pray. When I said, "Really?" He said that he was joking and that I needed to try to be less serious. I said, "I sure will, I promise." He laughed and said that even my answer was too serious.

The benches were all wet and the floor too, the piano stayed dry, but one window had opened slightly and the wall below it was soaked. We mopped up the water, dried the seats and gathered all of the song books that were wet to take them home to dry them in the oven. Pastor Mac's "Bonny Lassy" was not there, or she was hiding really good.

Things had dried pretty well by Sunday morning. Loaded down with the song books, we hiked up the hill to the church without falling even once. We were earlier this Sunday and there were only two people waiting on the front steps. One was Mr. Quick. Mac opened the door, made his critter inspection, and greeted the people as they came in. I got busy putting the books around the church and opening the curtains, some still wet from the rains.

Soon, the bus rolled up to the front door and then two cars, and the church was almost full when I suddenly felt off balance, and it seemed that I was going to fall down. I didn't know what was going on, then Pastor Mac yelled, "Everybody out! Everybody out of the buildin', it's a-movin'!"

A loud creaking and tearing noise started, and folks scrambled out the front door. Some women screamed, and the men yelled for everyone to hurry and get out! I stayed back with Mac as he herded the people out the door. The building was moving fast now, sideways, downhill, toward the swamp. I fell down twice, and we were the last to jump off the porch before it tore loose, sluing sideways and falling apart like a house of cards. The church continued its downhill slide, leaving pieces of itself along the way. All the while, Mr. Quick was busy taking pictures.

"Is everyone alright?" Mac called out. No one was hurt and we said a prayer right there to thank God for that. The church hit the first of the trees lining the swamp, splintered into a thousand pieces and collapsed with a dull thud. It took about an hour for everyone to leave before Pastor Mac and I were able to go down the hill, to pick up Bibles and hymn books and anything else of value. At the water's edge, the church was just a pile of lumber and broken glass. One end of the piano stuck up out of the swamp, and as we stood there, something moved. We stepped closer and saw Pastor Mac's "bonny lassy" slither from under the shattered piano.

Pastor Mac had tears in his eyes, and didn't say anything. He just stood there, staring at the rubble that was his life.

Chapter Five

You are going to have the light
just a little while longer.
Walk while you have the light,
before darkness overtakes you.

JOHN 12:35

That night Mac was very quiet as he fixed dinner. I wasn't hungry, but I ate anyway. I sat at the table looking at a hymn book. Suddenly I realized what I had done.

Mac came out of the bathroom and saw me crying, my face jammed into a dish towel. "There, lad," he comforted. "It'll be alright. We'll get another church . . . someplace . . ."

"No!" I bawled. "You don't understand! I caused that to happen! It's my f-f-fault . . . " I howled even louder.

"Now how in God's beautiful world could that be your fault, lad? The buildin' was almost 200 years old, and the foundation crumbled from the weight of all the people. She went a-slidin' down the slope, she did, all by herself." He put his big hand on my shoulder to comfort me.

I jumped up and said, "You don't know!" He looked at me, confused. "I told God that you needed a bigger church, and His light blinked 'yes.' He had to get rid of your old one for you to get a new, bigger one!"

My voice was coming in short gasps, and I couldn't stop crying. "But there's no way for us . . . *you* to get a new church. We . . . *you* don't have the money!" I sat down heavily in the chair.

He stepped around the table and sat across from me. He seemed older, and his eyes were sad, like the big dog at the grocery store. "There's one thing you haven't learned, my boy, and that is that God has a reason for everythin' He does."

I tearfully interrupted him, "Oh, sure, but what are we going to do now?"

He scratched his beard and said, "We're just going to let Him do what He said He would do—'*Never will I leave you; never will I forsake you.*' But we need to have faith, lad."

"What's 'four-shake you' mean?"

"No lad, it's 'forsake.'" He spelled it. "Take your Bible now and read Hebrews 13: 5. 'Forsake' means to give up on someone or abandon them, and He won't do that to us."

I went to bed but couldn't sleep because I didn't want to close my eyes and see my light. It had been nothing but trouble and I was the reason. I wished that it had never come around to mess things up. Now Pastor Mac had no church, we were about out of money, and we couldn't get a new church—or piano, or Bibles, or song books, or—*anything*. And it was all because of my light and my big mouth. My eyes closed and I slept. I didn't look to see if my light was there or not.

A knock at the door in the morning slowly woke me up. Pastor Mac was making breakfast, and he opened the door to two men who I saw in church the day before. They came in, and Mac poured coffee. They sat at the table and talked about the church sliding into the swamp, and asked Mac what he was going to do. I got up and took my clothes and went into the bathroom. They ignored me.

Pastor Mac was the only one who knew that I was the reason he lost his church. I stayed in the bathroom until I heard the door's glass rattling as it closed and the men left.

"Aye, me young friend," said Mac as I came out of the bathroom. "You be about ready for somethin' to eat?" I nodded and sat at the table.

"That was Carl and his brother, Edward—he'd be the tall one with the red hair. Those lads have a truck and we're going to gather up the wood and debris of the church and take it to Edward's place and burn it." He slid a plate of bacon and eggs in front of me. "We'll save what we can, but there won't be much, I'd be guessin.'"

He carried the men's cups and his breakfast plate to the sink and said, "But first we need to go into town and get us some gloves. It'll be hard work and rough on the hands."

"Would it be alright if I stayed here?"

"Why sure it would, lad. This be your home y'know. But I want you to listen first . . ." He sat back down with on one elbow on the table, rubbing his chin whiskers.

"Ye'll not be feelin' guilty about what happened to the old church. It is not your fault in any way, light or no light. It was indeed God's will, what He wanted. So you must nae be carryin' around a load of sorrow for somethin' that would have happened even if you'd never had your light, ye understand what I be sayin'?"

I nodded, but I still felt like I'd done it.

As he put on his coat, he said, "Oh, yes. Carl's misses is Hilda, the lady who played the piano," he went to the door. "She's the teacher at the Quickville School, and you and Wil are goin' to start school next week." He pointed at $3 laying on the table. "It's for you to buy pencils and paper and a notebook," he said before leaving.

It was the first time I'd ever been alone in the house, and it was quiet and cold. It made funny creaks and groans. I felt that it didn't want me there.

I washed up all of the dishes and cups and put them away. Then I put on my coat. I still had $2 from my work for Mr. Quick, so I left the $3 there for Pastor Mac. I looked around the small house and left. The rattling of the glass in the door was the only "Goodbye" to me.

I cut across the hills behind Quickville, keeping in the trees as much as possible. I stopped at the top of one rise and looked down at the town. An old gray truck moved slowly out of town northward toward where the church had stood. I was sure it was the three men who were going to cut up its busted-up remains.

By nighttime, I was well past the town and following the river to the south. I came to a large ranch that was totally dark. There were no cars or trucks. I figured it was some rich person's play ranch and that they probably lived in the city. I moved down the hill, slid under the white railed fence, and headed for the barn. A side door was unlocked and I pulled it open and peeked in. There were only two horses, and lots of empty stalls with beds of hay—perfect for me to sleep on.

I snuggled down into the hay and closed my eyes. There was my light. I was going to ignore it, but then as I thought about what had happened, I became angry.

"Look, God," I said aloud. The horses stirred and softly snorted. "I don't think what you did was a very good way to help Pastor Mac, by destroyin' his church." The light stayed steady. "At least I got him a little money to pay my way, and by me leavin', he'll not have to spend so much on food and stuff, and all you did was take away what he did have. All that *'You'll never leave me or forsake me'* stuff is just writin' in a book. It would have been better if I'd left you out of my life!"

The light remained unchanged. I grumbled and turned over and went to sleep.

I was in the big, round room again with the spring coiled around the inside. I was at the bottom, looking up at a big, hairy, black spider standing on the top of the coil. It began to bounce up and down, sending the spring bouncing down toward me, bringing the spider closer and closer with each effort. I knew that if the spider ever reached me, I'd be taken in it's claws and eaten like a bug.

The spider was one or two bounces from me when the barn doors creaked open and light flooded the inside of the barn. The horses snorted, whinnied, and shuffled around, anxious for food or exercise. I rolled over next to the stall and held my breath. I heard a man talking to the horses, the clatter of bridles, and the whomp of a saddle being put on, the shuffling of six feet as they left the barn.

I waited awhile and heard the horse and rider clomp away. I brushed the hay from my clothes and sneaked out the side door. I saw the man riding away over the rise, and out of sight.

I thought about that awful dream. It seemed to happen whenever I was in a bad spot. I began to imagine that if the spider ever actually reached me, I would die. I thought that I'd have to remember to ask Pastor Mac about that. Then remembered that I'd run off and I'd no longer have him to give me advice, or help, or breakfast, or anything else any more. I began to cry as I trudged along, heading nowhere.

I walked all day, slowly, aimlessly, until the twilight of evening crept up on me. I was nearing a small village alongside the river. It had a wharf longer than the entire town. One small riverboat was tied up to it. I went down out of the hills and shuffled along the town's only street. I hoped to find something to eat and drink. There was a space between two wooden buildings where trash cans and garbage cans were lined up. I went from one to the next lifting the lids and looking for some small bit to eat.

"Young man!" The voice startled me. I dropped the metal trash can lid, jumped back, the lid clanging loudly against the cans. A woman in a white apron stood with her hands on her hips staring at me. She was about the age of Mrs. Gilley, but her skin was dark brown like an Indian or maybe even Mexican.

"C'mon over here, boy, and don't be digging in those old trash cans, will you?"

She didn't sound angry so I went over to her hoping she'd offer me something to eat.

"You look hungry, and I got some left-overs from last night's dinner that you're welcome to, if you have a mind."

I was grateful and muttered, "Yes ma'am, I am a little hungry, but I'm willin' to work to pay you for the food."

"Well now, I don't remember anybody saying anything about paying for anything. This is left over food that'll get thrown into the river unless you want to eat it." She turned back into the building, giving me a wave to follow her in. I did.

It was a long, skinny kitchen with a big black stove along one wall and a shiny table in the middle with all sorts of pans, spoons, and cooking tools I didn't recognize. At the back was a sink with dishes and cups and glasses piled high alongside. The room was warm and smelled like food, soap, and garbage all at once.

"My name's Louise," she said while she fixed a plate of food. "What do we call you?"

"Ah . . . you can just call me Dor," I said.

"'Door' is a part of a house." She put the food on a small table in the corner and pulled a glass from a cupboard. "Don't you have a real name?"

"No, ma'am, that's about it."

"Well, 'Door,' come sit here and eat this while I finish up my work."

I sat down and began to eat. It was good and my mouth was too full to answer when she said, "You got any brothers or sisters, you know, like 'window' 'floor' or 'roof?'" She laughed and began to wash the dishes with steaming-hot water sending a fog above the sink.

I finished eating and felt really tired and sleepy—so sleepy that I couldn't keep my eyes open. I lay my head next to the plate and fell asleep. I dreamed I saw Pastor Mac running toward me calling my name. But he didn't see me and ran right past. I didn't yell to him. I was just trouble for him and his church.

A noise woke me only enough to hear Louise call out, "Skerv, I got one here for you!"

Through a haze, I saw a man who smelled of whiskey bend over. He looked at me for a long time.

"Lou, when did we start grabbin' babies?" He drooled the words through ragged, black teeth and a scruffy beard stained with a variety of colors from a variety of things.

"He ain't no baby, you miserable wharf rat. He's as fit as most of the others, and he's a lot older than he looks, I'd wager." She threw down the dish towel and said, "Go get your blasted wagon and get him out of here."

The man left, shoving the swinging doors so hard that they banged against the wall. Louise stood looking at me. "Sorry I got to do this to you, boy, but a lady's gotta make a dollar where she can these days, y'know."

I woke up again when the man lifted me into what seemed to be a wagon. I was curled up like a baby. He handed Louise some folded bills, and we left, the wagon's squeaking wheels keeping time as we went. Then everything went dark again.

I was in that little bit of time between being fully asleep and fully awake. Kind of a dark hallway between the two. I saw my light, a small, bright spot ahead in the blackness and was glad it was still with me. *I shall never leave you nor forsake you.* But I didn't want to talk to my light because it always got me in trouble. The darkness slowly became gray. I heard sounds, and realized that my head hurt and something was pounding in my ears. Unkie talked of the headaches he had in the morning after being out with his friends. I never had a headache, but I figured that this must be one. I didn't like it much.

Something hit me in the side, and I rolled over to see a big black man. He was bald and covered with black powdery stuff. His shirt had big muscles where there should have been sleeves. His face was covered with sweat. He had kicked me. He kicked me again.

"Hey! Stop it. That hurts," I cried.

"Y'all got work to do, young'n."

I was in a funny-looking room that had a big furnace all along one side and piles of coal on the other. The ceiling was low with lots of wood frames. It was hot and smelled bad. He grabbed my arm and snatched me to my feet. I was unsteady and realized that the room was moving. A loud, long whistle scared me and I jumped back. The man jerked my arm and dragged me to the first of a pair of doors in the furnace. He grabbed a shovel from the coal pile.

"Here, get to shovelin."

I scooped-up some coal and couldn't lift it off the floor without dumping some of it out. The black man was at the other door, shoveling great amounts into the roaring furnace.

"I can't do this, it's too heavy," I yelled.

"Get to shovelin' boy, or I'll use you to stoke the fire!" He grabbed the shovel and tossed the coal into the fire. "Jus' like dat!" He shoved the scoop at me and went back to his work.

I took up less than a full load and was just able to toss it into the furnace. I figured that if I did smaller loads, but more of them, he wouldn't fling me into the fire.

I was scared. Mad, too. I didn't know how I got there or how I'd get out of there. The one thing I figured-out was that somehow this was the boiler room of a river boat, and my anger made me keep putting coal into that flaming opening just as fast and as long as I could.

My shoulders ached and my hands were sore from the rough wood handle of the shovel. I saw he had gloves and that made me even madder.

"Hey, you!" I yelled.

He turned, leaned on his shovel, and said "What you want, kid?"

"If you want me to keep doin' this, you'd better get *me* some gloves too, mister!"

He reached over to the wall, and tossed me a dirty, black pair.

"That's better," I said, and put them on. They were too big, but might keep me from getting blisters. I shoveled some more, still mad.

"Hey, you!" I yelled again.

"What you want *now*?"

"You got a name?"

He grinned at me. "Boy, you got a lotta grit, ain't you!"

"Well?" I pressed.

"Name's Jason," he muttered.

Jason wasn't as mean as he acted. Sure, he was big and strong, but now I didn't think he'd really throw me into the fire.

It seemed like I'd been shovelin' that dirty old black coal for a whole day, and the pile that I'd started with had gotten a lot smaller. Jason left me alone, so the time went fast. A loud bell scattered my thoughts. I leaped away from the roaring furnace in surprise.

"What's that?" I asked Jason.

"One bell means we're dockin' someplace. Y'all can stop stokin' now." He tossed his scoop into the pile of coal and reached up for a ladder on the back wall. "You stay here now, boy. I'll be back with some eats." He disappeared through a square opening in the overhead.

The room was gloomy. A single bulb hung in the middle, but it was black with coal dust. With nothing else to do, I slid a crate over, found a pile of rags in a corner, and used one to clean off the old bulb. I shoved the crate back against the wall and discovered a broom. I swept the walkway free of chunks of coal and a thick layer of coal dust, then wiped-down the front of the furnace using water from a fire bucket in a holder on one of the deck supports.

I was using a wet cloth to wipe my face, arms and hands when Jason returned.

"Gawd Amighty, boy!" His eyes were wide as he looked around the boiler room, mouth hanging open.

"Wot's wrong wit you? You crazy or sumpin'?"

"What you mean?"

"Boss man goin' to want us to do this alla time now! And how we goin' sleep here with that light so bright? Y'ever think of that?"

I said that I didn't want to work in a place so dirty. Mumbling and shaking his head, he handed me a plate of food and a bottle of soda pop, and hurried back up the ladder.

I pulled the packing crate out, sat down and picked up the spoon. I remembered what Pastor Mac said. *"Aye lad, we'll thank our Lord for our food before every meal and before we take a bite, alright?"*

I bowed my head, closed my eyes and prayed, "Dear Father in heaven, thank you for this food. I sure am hungry, and I promise I'll do my best here on this boat if you'll kind of watch out for me, O.K.? Amen."

I was just about finished eating whatever it was that was on my plate, when Jason came back down the ladder.

"Boy, the boss man wanna see you. Now!"

I started up the ladder and then stopped, "Where is he, Jason?"

"You'll know, boy. You'll know."

Chapter Six

**I have come into the world as a light,
so that no one who believes in me
should stay in darkness.**

JOHN 12:46

I came up through a square hole into a room with boxes, machines, cans of something, and bales of cotton all stacked around the walls. There was only a little path between all the stuff. It was as dark as the boiler room, but it smelled a lot better. Light came from one end of the place, so I headed for that. I heard a growl like a big animal and then loud cursing and a banging noise, like an angry bear was trying to get out. Or in. It scared me, so I peeked around a big box and saw that the back of the room was open, the river went off into the distance in a big curve, and the sun was shining. A man in a funny-looking blue coat was yelling at two men shoving a wooden crate into the room. The man yelled, then beat on the crate with his cane.

"Git on with it, you lazy sacks of swamp scum!" The men pushed as hard as they could, and I wondered why "blue coat" didn't help. I ran over between the men and began to shove as hard as I could on the big box. It slid with a screech into a space between cotton bales and stopped against another box. The men just looked at me like I was weird.

"Stop yer dawdlin' you worthless buggers. There's more to be loaded!" He slammed the cane against the big box, looked at me, and made an awful face.

"You scruffy little pile of chicken bones, don't you ever do nothin' I don't tell you to do, or I'll whup you 'til your lousy hide falls off!"

"Yes, sir."

"So, you're the dirty little wart that's got the black stoker so upset?"

"I guess so, sir. All I did was . . ."

"Shattup!" He slammed the cane against the crate again. "Nobody told you to talk back to me. You'd better learn, and learn fast, that I'm doin' the talkin'. You're doin' the workin'. You got that?"

"Yes, sir, I.."

"Shattup!"

I walked right over to him, looked him in the eyes and said, "Pastor Mac said that I should be treated with respect, and that I should treat everyone else with respect, but you're makin' it kinda hard, sir."

"Shattup!" He slammed the crate again. He looked down at the floor, shaking his head.

"You say you know Pastor Mac at the Kirkcaldy church?"

I didn't say anything, just nodded, so that he wouldn't whack his cane again.

He relaxed, "How is old Jamison these days?"

I didn't say anything. I just looked at him.

"Dag nabbit, boy!" he yelled. "When I ask you a question, you better give me an answer, but fast, or I'll make raw liver out of that blasted bony backside of yours! You got that?"

I nodded again. "He's lost his church. The foundation crumbled and it slid down the hill into the swamp."

Blue coat sort of sagged, looking down at the floor. "That old shack of a church finally fell apart, did it?"

I nodded.

"Folly me," he said as he walked past me and around the crate to a small open door. Slamming his cane down, he sat heavily behind a desk made from a crate that still had shipping labels stuck on it. A wooden chair with missing slats creaked like it was in pain when he sat and pointed to a smaller box. I sat down.

"I'm the captain of the *Killdeer*. What be your name?"

"Walker. Actually, Dorky Walker, sir."

"Very well, Walker, you best know that you've not started out on the right foot here, and you're a problem for me. You're too puny to be of much good on this barge."

"What's 'pooney'?" I asked.

He reached for the cane, stopped and yelled, "That means you're five pounds short of bein' a half-ounce. You got not enough muscle to raise your eyebrows. You're skinny, weak, and I've paid more than what 10 of the likes of you would be worth!"

"Well, Pastor Mac said I'm a hard-worker and smart . . . and . . . and, a blessin'!" I stood, grabbed the cane and slammed it down on the crate just as he'd done so many times. "And I don't like talkin' to someone who won't tell me his name." I tossed the cane down in front of him. "You got a name, 'Captain?'"

Blue coat leaned back in his chair. He was quiet while a small smile turned into a big grin. He finally laughed out loud, "I be Hannah, Captain Jonathan Hannah," he said. "You're sure feisty. You sure you're not Jamison's son?"

I remembered something that he said that bothered me. "You paid more than I'm worth?"

He was lighting his pipe and talked out the side of his mouth, "Yep. Old Louise took me 'round the bend on you."

I leaned forward on the crate and looked him in the eyes. "She *sold* me? To you?

"That's about it, boy, but it'll be the last sale for her and that river scum, Skerv." He got up. "Folly me."

He led me up some stairs to a cabin. The steering place was on the left. There was a greasy wall, a small kitchen with an old black stove, and a sagging table nailed to the back wall.

"If you don't know how to cook and make coffee and sandwiches, you'd better just crawl off somewheres and hide yourself, 'cause that's the only thing I can figure for you to do to earn your keep. Got it?"

"Pastor Mac learnt me to do some cookin', and sure, I can make sandwiches and such."

"Well, we'll see. You can sleep on that pad under the table, and when I'm at the helm, you keep my coffee cup full and be ready with whatever else I want. You'll make breakfast and lunch for the crew when we're underway, and bring me food when I tell you.

"Is that steering place, the 'helm'?"

"Well now, what else could it possibly be, for Lord's sake? Boy, you never been on a riverboat afore?" Before I could answer, he went on. "It's called the wheelhouse too, and you'll stay inside the cabin whilst we are in port. I don't want to see you wandering around on deck unless we're underway and only then if I've been provided with my needs. Got that?"

"Yes, sir."

"Another thing," he yelled. "You'll be answering me 'Aye, sir' or 'Aye, Captain.' And this vessel is the *Killdeer*, so if you hear someone yelling that name, it's for us. If you're gonna be a riverboatman, ya gotta talk like a riverboatman."

"What's a '*Killdeer*?'"

He ignored my question, stomped off down the stairs, mumbling to himself something I couldn't hear. I looked around the small, dirty kitchen and began to pick up trash and things that didn't belong there. I went through the drawers and found plates, cups and glasses, and knives and forks. A wooden ice box on the floor was full of bread, eggs, pieces of some kind of meat, bacon, and a chunk of ice.

I cleaned off the top of the stove and the table and put down some newspaper that I found tossed into a corner. I laid out the meat. It didn't smell real good and had a sort of scum on the outside. I scraped that off and wrapped the slimy mess in another piece of newspaper. I found some beans in a bag and put them into a pot of water that I poured from the ice box and chopped-up some of the meat. On the inside, without the scum, it smelled like it might be ham.

I opened a drawer at the end of the table and found some onions and other things—one looked like garlic. I chopped an onion and half of a garlic thing and put them in with the beans, all the while repeating, "'Aye captain. Aye, sir.'". In a little while, the pot began to boil, so I slowed the fire and tossed in the meat.

"Lordy, boy, what're cookin' up here?" It was Jason, up from the engine room. "I could smell it clean down in the hell hole!"

"Hi Jason, I'm gettin' some food cooked-up. Do you know where there is some bowls or plates or spoons or somethin' like that?"

He walked past the stove, sniffing the air and going "Ummm, ummm!" and pulled open a section of the wall. Inside was what I needed.

"Y'all don't mind if'n I have a little taste of that in the pot, huh?" I gave him a spoon and said, "Sure, go ahead. You'll be my tester. What time should I have this ready for the crew?"

Jason tasted the beans, cracked a huge grin. "Ain't no crew on nights we is in port. It's just the captain, you, and me, and we eat at sundown."

"How 'bout the other meals?" I asked.

"Well," he took another taste of the beans. "Ummm! Breakfast is at sunup, and we usually has some sandwich ready up here for whenever we can get to them in the daytime."

I took the spoon away from him and got a mean look for my effort. "You'll have to wait 'til sunset for your dinner, Jason, jus' like the rest of us!"

He stomped out mumbling about it being too long a wait.

At sundown, I called, "Aye, Capt. Hannah, your dinner is ready!" I heard a grumble from below and he came up the ladder, Jason right at his heels.

"Ye don't fetch me up with a yell like I was some sort of animal. I'll be served in my . . ." He looked at the bowls of steaming beans and ham, and walked slowly to the table, sniffing the smells. Jason almost ran into him in his haste to get to the food.

"Set down, aye, sir, and I'll get you some bread."

He looked at me, mumbling something about 'aye, sir' and dropped himself onto a packing crate, still sniffing the beans.

Jason and I sat down and I said, "Aye, captain, would you say grace, please?"

"I'll not eat at the crew's table with the blasted crew," he yelled, looking hard at Jason. "And I'll not be told what to do and when to do nothing on my own ship. Take your vittles below, stoker."

Jason looked sad, said "Aye, sir," picked up his bowl and left.

"I'll abide your presence, Walker, but only to inspect your work . . ." His voice lowered. "Dear Lord, we thank ye for this food and pray that You'll bless our miserable bodies and souls as we partake. Amen."

We ate in silence, the only sounds were the captain's slurping and lip-smacking.

While I was cleaning up the kitchen I found a dictionary in a drawer. I looked-up "Killdeer" and found that it is a water bird found inland—like where we were, and it had a weird cry like, "kill-deeeer".

A loud noise woke me up early in the morning.

"Here's your stores!" A man left a big box at the top of the ladder and disappeared.

"Stores?" I rubbed the sleep out of my eyes and pulled the flaps open. There was all sorts of food in the box; eggs, bacon, corn, flour, and some things I didn't recognize. I shoved the box under the table and went to the bathroom where I splashed water in my face and under my arms and tried to get myself clean enough to be the riverboat's cook. It was still dark. A lantern in the wheelhouse sent shafts of light flashing back and forth across the tiny kitchen with the rocking of the boat.

I went to work making the coffee and getting the crew's breakfast ready. I felt like the most important person on the boat, and it was a good feeling—at least until the captain came up the ladder yelling and pounding his cane like he was killin' a mess of beetle bugs.

He quieted when he saw that I was up and fixing the morning meal, "Get me my coffee now!" he muttered, and stomped off to the wheelhouse.

I took the coffee and a muffin with grape marmalade to the wheelhouse. The Captain was leaning over the chart table reading a Bible.

"Aye, captain," I said softly. "Here's your coffee."

"Boy, ye don't say 'aye' unless you're meaning 'yes,'" he growled. "It's just 'aye' or 'captain' or 'sir' without putting them together unless you mean 'aye, sir' or 'aye, Captain.' Do ye understand that?"

"Aye, captain, sir!"

He put his head in his hands and muttered something about 'needing help, Lord.'

"Walker," he called out as I was leaving. "You made me remember my friend, Jamison MacAndrew, and his name brought back memories I'd let slip from me somewhere along this river." His voice was kind of quiet. "He's a good man. A holy man. He's about the best friend any man—or woman—on this old earth, could ever expect to find."

"Aye, sir, captain." I replied. And he gave me a look like he was going to yell at me, but he didn't.

He lifted his Bible, looked at it for a minute, and continued. "He taught me much, and I let it drift away from me whilst I kept my mind on the runnin' of this here boat." He straightened up and said, "I want us to have a Bible readin' the first night of our first day in whatever port we might land, and I want you and the crew to gather on the main deck for it. Do ye understand?"

Before I could answer, he said, "When I was readin' the Word and followin' God's commands, things were going well for me. I got this here boat . . ."

"How did you do that?" I interrupted.

"Well, she was owned by a Mr. Kildeere and I was runnin' her up and down the river for him. This was just about the time I met Jamison MacAndrew and learned about faith in the Lord." He looked to see if I was listening.

"Things were going fine," he continued, "and when Mr. Kildeere up and died, he gave me this here boat. He had no family. A lawyer in Evansville did up all the papers for it to be legal and all, and I got the *Killdeer*." He put the Bible down. "I got so busy runnin' up and down this here river, I plum forgot about the Bible, the Father, the Son, and the Holy Ghost, and even Jamison. Then you came along—I guess you was sent by God—and it all came back to me. Now I want to get back to where I was."

"You said Father, Son, and what?"

He slowly re-lit his pipe and said, "God sent his only Son to this earth as a man to give sinners like us a chance for eternal life in Heaven with the Father, God. Those who believe have the Holy Ghost or Holy Spirit, if you prefer, in them, leading and directing them. The Son is God and so is the Holy Ghost."

"How can God be three things? That's impossible," I said.

"No," he answered. "Not impossible. Look at this old river. She's three things; she has banks or levees to hold her on her course, a muddy bottom to keep her from soakin' into the dirt, and of course, the water. Take away any one and she'll no longer be a river."

I understood that. "And like this riverboat too," I said. "It's got a hull, and a wheelhouse and an engine. without any one, she'd no more be a riverboat, right?"

He just smiled at me, "Aye, lad."

For the next two years, he had Bible study at every port, but I tried to make up reasons I couldn't be there. The captain stopped yelling and banging his cane down on things, and it got to be almost pleasant on that old boat, cruising up and down the river, loading and unloading and him talking about the Bible and God and Jesus. If there was no loading or other work to do on Sundays, the Captain would go find a local church. In all that time he said he never heard a preacher as good as Pastor Mac. I still didn't go back to talking to my light.

I was learnin' about the river, and steering the riverboat upstream and downstream, and was almost ready to learn how to bring her up to a dock. Finally, on our last trip to Barriston, I brought the *Killdeer* up to the dock nicely, and even the captain said I done good.

We were there for three days, unloading and loading cargo for the trip back downriver.

On the third day, as I was fixing the breakfast, I felt the boat pull away from the dock and heard the captain hollering and the whistle screaming its warnings as the riverboat moved slowly downstream.

We were on the river two days. The captain stayed at the helm all the time, except for a little while when me or a deckhand would hold the wheel to let the captain go to the bathroom or study a river chart, penciling things on it.

Going downstream, we would make the regular run in two days, but it took four days going upstream. I didn't know how the captain could stay awake all that time and be able to watch the loading and unloading as well.

I had the meals ready long before time, every time, and hadn't been yelled at hardly at all for months. We just kept steaming up and down the river, carrying all sorts of things. All the while, the captain was getting pretty tired. Most every time I brought him his food when we were in port, I'd find him asleep at the chart table or his head down on the old crate desk.

It was my third year on the *Killdeer* and Capt. Hannah said that he was raising my pay to a full $5 a month. I didn't know what I was going to do with all that money, I had only spent a little of the $4 a month I'd earned for some clothes and shoes since I came aboard the boat. I figured that it wouldn't be long before I was rich, so I kept it all hidden away in a empty coffee sack in the boat's galley. With my next month's pay, I'd have to get a whole 'nother coffee bag.

It was a very dry summer that year, and the river was low. Capt. Hannah had to keep the riverboat clear of sandbars—he called them 'snags'—and he made me his Bow Watch. I stood at the front of the boat and pointed to where I saw snags or floating trees and stuff.

The winter came on all of a sudden and the rain poured day and night. It never stopped, and the river ran muddier than ever. Big trees and pieces of houses went floating by, and the old riverboat jerked and shuddered at her Hawkinsville dock. The water got up to the bottom of the pier and waves slapped the back of the boat so hard that the whole aft deck was under a shower of muddy river water all the time. That made loading the cargo real hard, and the Captain was madder than usual because it took so long. I just did my work and tried to stay clear of him.

We went through snow storms too, but we always got our cargo to wherever it was supposed to go. This was teaching me more and more about being a riverboatman, but as the river rose up and the water rushed faster and faster, and got to look just like mud, I worried about doing something really wrong that would wreck the boat. But the captain didn't seem worried about that Like a father teaching his son, he gave me more and more to do.

We pulled out of Hawkinsville one dark, windy morning, and headed downstream for Millton. It continued to rain harder than any rain I'd ever seen. It made the water look like it was alive with jittery fish, and I couldn't see ahead more than a few yards.

One day, the Captain didn't want me to be on the bow, so I was in the galley getting food ready for the day. The boat was shaking like a mare bothered by flies, and the wind rattled every part of the old boat. I heard a bang, and Capt. Hannah said something—it sounded like "Walker!"—so I went into the wheelhouse. He was on the deck on his side with his arm twisted up behind him. His eyes looked funny, like he was just waking up. He was jerking like he was really cold, and his mouth was moving but nothing came out.

I yelled for the deckhands and grabbed the wheel. The boat was headed right for the shoreline and a tangled mess of tree roots that would snag her like a spider grabbing a bug. I spun the big wheel to port just as hard as I could and signaled the stoker for more steam. The boat shuddered and rolled from side to side like it was doing some kind of voodoo dance. Slowly she swung her nose away from the shore. We skimmed past the knotted tree roots with just a couple of feet to spare. I steered her back to the middle of the river. The two deckhands came in, soaking wet and drunk.

"The captain done took sick," I shouted at them. "Take him into my bunk and see what you can do for him!"

They suddenly got serious-looking and sort of dragged him back into the galley. They knew that they'd be out of a job if the captain up and died.

An especially skinny place in the river came up. It made a bend, then widened out and ran straight for a couple of miles. Once we were around the bend, I took a minute to close my eyes. For only the second time since I left Pastor Mac's house, I was looking to my light, and there it was! "God," I said. "Is that You?" The light blinked off, then on. It was true that He never left me. I left Him, but now I was glad to be back. I opened my eyes, feeling better. I knew I wasn't going to have to do this all by myself.

The river ahead was all jumbled-up like a bed full of squirrels under mussed-up covers. The water got even darker, and the rain made it hard to see past the white bow railing. Sometimes I had to stick my head out the side door to see where to go. Soon, I was soaking wet and shivering cold.

I heard the call of a Killdeer bird.

I took a quick look at the river map and saw that the next town with a riverboat landing and big enough to have a real doctor, would be Quickville. It looked to be just a few miles downriver. I hoped I would be able to see it in the heavy rain.

Killdeer was going faster than I'd ever seen her go. The river was taking her to the races! I figured I'd have to turn upstream when I got to Quickville, and head for the dock against the river's current. It was going to be hard, but I'd seen Capt. Hannah do it before, and I learn pretty good.

I yelled to the deck crew to watch for the Quickville dock and holler when they saw it. Then I yelled over my shoulder to Jason in the engine room to be ready for getting up all the steam he could when we made the turn upstream. I heard him yell back, "Aye, sir!" That made me feel real good inside. "Aye, sir!"—to me!

Through the side window of the pilothouse, I saw the place where crews repaired the jetty that gave away some three years or more ago. Just then the crewmen hollered at me that Quickville dock lay just ahead. I yelled to Jason, "Gimme all you got, Stoker!" I barely heard his "Aye, sir!"

I spun the wheel hard to port and watched as the *Killdeer* began to shake and bounce in the cross-current. When we were sideways to the river's flow, she seemed to be traveling faster than she had been when going ahead. I saw the Quickville pier tear on by. Finally, the old riverboat had her nose pointed back into the current and she slowed down, then began to move upstream a little at a time—so slowly I thought I knew how a snail must feel. The old riverboat was shuddering and shaking like those Hawaiian huli-huli dancers do, but she was slowly getting on back to the Quickville dock.

"One of you get ready on the moorin' line," I hollered. "And the other get Captain Hannah onto the pier and go lookin' for a doctor!" I heard a "Aye!" from one of them.

There were big bollards on the pier to tie onto. They looked like a pair of great big, black, iron frogs sitting back to back. A big rope is tossed over them when front the boat is close to the dock. The line holds the boat, and she swings up against the pier nice like.

I'd watched Capt. Hannah a lot of times docking the boat, even in terrible-fast current like this. I did it like he done before, and I saw the pilings and fenders slide alongside *Killdeer*, just like he done it.

"Line's secure!" came a shout. I eased off on the power. *Killdeer* nudged the dock easily, and stopped.

I saw that my hands were shaking and I felt like I had a stomach ache. I squeezed my eyes closed to keep from crying with relief. I leaned hard on the wheel and felt it shudder in the raging currents under the boat. I had my eyes closed, so I prayed, "God, thank you for making me able to get this here boat safely tied up here. And please, God help the captain get better." The light was there as before, and it made me feel good that I wasn't alone, even when nobody else was around.

Chapter Seven

Show me your ways, LORD,
teach me your paths.

PSALM 25:4

The sky got so dark it looked like the middle of the night. The rushing river made the boat jerk and snap against the mooring lines that held her. Moaning and cracking noises came from somewhere outside. I went to the side wheelhouse door to see what was happening. Just then there was a horrible grinding noise and the boat rolled up on her side. I was thrown across the wheelhouse and crashed through the door on the other side. I fell toward the cold, black, wild water. The last thing I saw was *Killdeer* laying on her side and swinging out into the river. The whole Quickville dock was being dragged along, its boards cracking and snapping and pilings shooting up into the air like wooden rockets.

Then I hit the water.

I was in that gray place between being asleep and being awake. I could hear things somewhere like they were far away, but I was still dreaming. It wasn't the spider dream. This time I was being dragged along the river bottom, and up the rocks of the jetty. Then Capt. Hannah yelled at me and banged his cane on a rock. Sparks flew from the cane as I heard him yell, "You lost my boat, Walker!" Then he whacked the rock again. "You wrecked *Killdeer!*" I tried to say that I got her to the dock okay, but the dock broke away. It wasn't my fault . . . was it Aye sir? "Don't 'Aye sir' me, you 'gator-brained sack 'o chicken lips!" He was sliding off into the distance until I couldn't hear him any more.

I could just make out the light in me and said, "God, don't let the captain be mad at me, please?" The light blinked off and on, and faded away as I started to wake up.

"Well, lad, this is becomin' a habit with ye, it is." I could hear Pastor Mac's voice as clear as could be, but I couldn't see him. Everything was just a foggy blur.

"You've been gone a fair long time, m'boy, and I've been worryin' myself about you, but you look a'right. You've grown into a fine young man, ye have." His voice seemed to be getting farther and farther away, and I tried to call out to him to stay, but I couldn't talk. The blackness came back and there in the center of it was my light.

Then Jesus told them, "You are going to have the light just a little while longer. Walk while you have the light, before darkness overtakes you. The man who walks in the dark does not know where he is going."

JOHN 12:35

I prayed I would be able to see again and talk with Pastor Mac, and see that Capt. Hannah was well, and that we could all be together. The light went off, then back on, and I knew God heard me. He'd make things okay again.

I was back in Pastor Mac's house in the old bunk bed, with the soft pillow and the blankets pulled up over my head. I could hear his soft snoring rumbling through the room. The dream faded, but I could still hear the sounds of Pastor Mac sleeping.

I opened my eyes expecting the foggy blur like before, but I could see that I was in somebody's house. Flowered curtains rustled softly as a light wind passed through and around them and I heard crickets in the night. There was a sweet smell. To my left, a bunch of roses sat on a bedside table. Roses! I never had roses—or any kind of flowers by my bed, ever. Beyond the flowers I saw Pastor Mac slumped in a chair, his mouth was open and his beard moved up and down as he snored. I wanted so to talk to him, but didn't want to wake him.

I tried to turn onto my side. It hurt all over. My legs ached like I'd been climbing 100 stairs, my arms felt as if I'd lifted 100 tons of cargo. I remembered the *Killdeer* being torn away with the pier and the terrible cold, choppy water of the river when I fell in. Pain shot through my chest with my smallest movement, and my throat felt like I'd eaten a barrel of gravel from a Quickville road. But I knew that I was alive, and that was good.

I tried to rise up in the bed, but it felt like 100 nails were sticking into my back and shoulders. I guess I made a noise because Pastor Mac made a loud snorting sound and stood up, looking all worried.

"Lay back now, lad," he said. "You've had a bit of a run-in with that old river again, son." His hair was all mussed up and he had a beard where he was usually shaved. His eyes were all puffy and red around the edges. He looked tired—real tired.

I suddenly felt bad that I had run away from him. I thought I might cry. He's the only one who ever saw me cry, except for my mother. I said, "Pastor Mac, I'm sorry I went away. But I was causin' you trouble, and costin' you money, and I was the reason you lost your church . . ."

"That'll do, lad," he pulled the chair over to the bed and sat down. "That's all in the past. You're back, and it's mighty glad I am that you are."

"How'd I get here? And where am I? And how is Capt. Hannah? And . . ."

"Whoa, lad! Not so much so fast." He brushed his hair back with his hand and said, "First, you were hit by the riverboat's mast as the old boat turned over, and you were knocked unconscious. It took three men to drag you up on the jetty and bring you here." He shifted his weight in the chair. "'Here' is my house in Quickville. And about Capt. Hannah, well, he's gone, m'boy."

"Gone? When is he coming back?"

"No, lad. He's gone to be with the Lord God. He's in a better place, and Heaven is a better place now that he's there."

"But my light!" I was scared. Again, I was about to cry. "I asked that he be safe and well, and my light said 'Yes.' And now he's *dead*?"

"Aye, lad. He is safe and well in the arms of Jesus. He was a good Christian man, and it's the very best we can expect, to be in heaven when our time down here has run out, y'know."

I closed my eyes and felt the burning, wet tears leaking out and onto my cheeks. How could everything go so wrong? I've lost the captain, and I lost his boat, and now I have nothing. I wiped my eyes on the sheet and asked Pastor Mac, "Are Jason and the deck crew alright?"

"Sure and they are, lad. Johnny and Pete carried the good captain here and didn't see what happened to the boat until later. The *Killdeer's* alayin' on her side on a sand spit, parts of the dock still draggin' at her carcass. I 'spect she'll be there for a long while, now that the river is lowerin'"

There was a soft tap on the door and Mrs. Gilley came in, carrying a tray. "Ah, m'love," said Mac. "Dorky, you'll not be knowin' this, but this wonderful lady became my wife some two years ago."

She looked younger than she did before, and she was actually smiling, something I never thought I'd ever see her do. "Hullo, ma'am," I croaked. She smiled more and sat the tray alongside the bed. I saw a sandwich and a bowl of soup.

"I'd imagine that you are a very hungry young man, Dor." She used the nickname Wil gave me.

"Yes, ma'am." I tasted the soup, but it burned my throat. I ate the sandwich. It was really good.

While I ate, Mac told me, "After you went away, I spent days lookin' for ye, but had no luck." He slid the chair next to the bed. "All at once, I lost my church and my best friend and helper. Then Mason Quick came to me and offered the old *Quickville Courier* warehouse for my new church. Many townsfolk came and worked many hours makin' it into the new Kirkcaldy Christian Church." He took the empty plate from my hands, scratched at his beard, and smiled. "Mrs. Gilley and young Willie came every day and worked on makin' it a proper church." He smiled and lowered his voice, like he was going to tell me a secret, "Even Johnny Smallhead worked hard makin' new benches, and lovely they are!"

"This all happened because of the old church being all broken up?"

"Aye, lad, sure. It was God workin' in his mysterious way." He spoke quietly again. "Then things began to happen fast. Mrs. Gilley worked at the new church every day and I finally realized that I couldn't live happily without her in my life. I was sure amazed when she said that she felt the same. Earlier that year, her husband had been shot and killed whilst attemptin' to rob a store in Biloxi. We we were married the same week that we had the first service in the new church." His smile broadened, "I'm a very happy man, lad."

I felt a new sadness as I realized that by running away, I missed all of the fun and excitement of the new church, the wedding, being with my friend, Wil, and all the townspeople working to make Mac a new church. But I also realized that, by running away, I learned very much, found Capt. Hannah, and learned how to run a riverboat. I wasn't sure which of the two I would have wanted to give up if I had the choice. That thought drifted away as sleep again took over.

My dreams were all mixed up and goofy, and I sort of half awoke and then went back to sleep many times. I was about to wake up and I saw my light, a small bright dot in the darkness. I said, "Are you here with me, God?" The light blinked off, then on. "I can't do anythin' right, God. I went away, and I should have stayed. I should have been here to help with the new church. I don't know what to do now." A thought came into my mind. It was just sort of there, without me thinking about it. "I need to go to the *Killdeer*, right God?" The light blinked off, on.

I awoke to see Wil standing by my bed. He was in a white T-shirt and jeans. His hair was longer and he looked older than I remembered.

"Dor, my man," he said. "You look terrible, man. What you been doin' and where you been?"

"Hey, Wil," I croaked. "I been on the river. Runnin' a riverboat up and down. It was hard, but I learned a lot."

"Wow! A real riverboat?"

"Yep, the *Killdeer*." I pushed myself up on one elbow and put my legs over the side of the bed. I hurt all over, but I needed to get up. "Wil, I need to get to the *Killdeer* to get something off of her. Will you help me do it?"

"Are you sure it's okay for you to get up?"

"I don't even know if I can, but I've got to try to get to the boat."

"I hear it's layin' on its side out there in the river with big hunks of wood stickin' out of it all over. I don't know how we'll get there, but sure, I'll help you."

"Her," I said.

"What?"

"You call a boat 'her' or 'she' but never 'it.'"

"Wow, man. You did learn a lot, didn't you!" he said.

Wil looked in the drawers and in the closet and found my clothes, all washed and ironed. I felt weak and funny-like. The room seemed to keep moving, and I stumbled around just like the drunken crewmen on the *Killdeer* did.

"Ma and Pastor Mac aren't here. They'll be home in a couple of hours," said Wil. "How long this goin' to take?"

"I don't know," I said. "I guess it depends on how hard it is to get out to the boat."

Every step hurt bad, and by the time we got to the front door, I wondered if maybe this wasn't a very smart thing to do, but I had to get my coffee bags off of the *Killdeer* before someone else found them and took all the money I'd saved.

On the front porch, I got so dizzy that I had to sit on the step until it went away. We reached the river in just a few minutes, and I had to sit down again. "We won't ever get there if I have to keep restin'." I told Wil.

The resting gave us time to talk. Wil had been going to school ever since I left and learned to read and write. He passed every class. I felt real good for him.

We walked along the river bank a little ways, and I saw the *Killdeer* for the first time since she wrecked. She looked like a pile of firewood stacked up high and dry 'way out in the river.

"How we goin' to get to her?" I asked Wil.

"If we go to the other side of the river, we won't have so far to go. Maybe we can make a raft or something from the junk over there."

We walked down to the new railroad bridge, crossed over, and made our way along the river bank to the spot closest to where *Killdeer* lay.

"Look here!" said Wil.

A large section of the dock had broken away and was aground on the bank. "It looks almost like a boat!" said Wil. "And we can use those pieces of board over there for paddles," I said.

Capt. Hannah taught me that rivers flow slower around the inside of a bend and faster at the outside—the biggest curve—of a turn in the river. *Killdeer* was on a sand bar at the inside of a curve and the water flowed much slower there than on the other side of the river. Wil led us the right way. It wouldn't be too hard to paddle against the slow-moving current between the shore and the grounded *Killdeer*, that is, if we could get the section of dock loose from the sandy river bank.

We saw that someone stretched a heavy rope out to the boat and had it tied to a tree on the bank. "Somebody's been here before us."

"Yup," said Wil. "There's marks in the sand where something has been dragged."

"Oh,oh," I said, "The cargo!" I also thought of the two coffee sacks with my money that were surely gone now, even though I had them pretty well hidden.

"Nothin' here now," said Wil. "I guess now there's no reason to get on it . . . *her*!"

I still needed to see for sure if the money was there, "There might be somethin' left. Let's go take a look, okay?"

The piece of the pier moved easily when we pryed against its end. We slid it into the water and used the boards for paddling. Partly submerged, it floated off toward the *Killdeer*. Wil scrambled on at the last minute and got his pants soaked. The rope was fixed so it held the raft from the current, and it was easy to paddle to the wreck. We climbed aboard *Killdeer* to find everything scattered around like a giant madman had picked up the boat and shook it. We made our way to the front of the cabin and saw that all of the cargo had been dragged through the boat and taken away. In the galley, the stove was torn from its mounting and lay on its side. The door hung open and pots and pans were all over the place. We'd have to move the stove to get to where my money bags were. I felt happy that they were covered and hidden, but wondered how Wil and I were going to move that big old iron stove. We tried to shove it, but it was just too heavy. We looked for something we could use to lift or pry it up, but with the big legs dug into the deck, it looked pretty impossible.

"What y'all doin' here?" A big, booming voice scared us and we about jumped out of our skins. I wanted to run but a huge man blocked the way out.

"Hey, there, Mr. Walker!"

It was Jason. The big black man was still dressed in the clothes he wore when the boat wrecked, all dirty-gray from coal dust.

The fright had made my voice go all squeaky as I said, "Jason! Man, it's good to see you. What are you doin' still here?"

"Well, when the boat went over, I was kind of trapped down there in the engine room with them hot boilers, and I knew they'd blow if the cold water got to 'em. I went and closed all the hatches as tight as I could and just hung on!"

"That musta been some ride," said Wil.

"Oh, Jason, this is my friend Wil. His mom is married to Pastor Mac now."

"Ah, well that's mighty fine, young man. Your new daddy is a great man and you'll do well to try to be just like him. Now, like I said, what you two doin' here?"

I didn't know if I should tell Jason about the money. I finally decided that Wil and I couldn't get it by ourselves, so I'd have to trust Jason. "There's a loose board and a cubby hole under the galley window, next to the stove. I have somethin' in there, but now the stove is alayin' right on top of it and me and Wil can't budge that big old thing."

Jason went to the stove, looked around it, "Under there?" he asked. The big man squatted down beside the stove, grabbed its side, and just stood up! The stove raised up like it was made of paper. He slid it aside and sat it back down.

Wil and I cheered and Jason looked right proud. I hurried to the loose board, popped it open and looked into an empty space. My coffee bags were gone. My money was gone. I sat down and tried to hide my tears.

"You boys come with me. And Mr. Walker, don't you go a cryin' y'hear?"

He crawled through the opening that was once where the ladder led down into the engine room, and we followed. I was still sniffling and felt like a big old mule had kicked me right in the belly.

All the loose coal was piled at one end, and there was a bed made up in the middle of the room. A small fire burned in one of the tilted boiler chambers, its door hanging open. A gasoline lantern hung above a small table and chair. Even though they sat at an angle, looked right comfortable. There were clothes neatly folded atop a box, and a pair of shiny shoes. A pile of cotton bags were arranged as a bed where daylight shone through an open hatch. "This here where you're livin'?" asked Wil.

"This is my home for now," said Jason. "Without no boat or no job, I got no money for a place. I spend most days lookin' for work, but none so far, and I'm able to live here okay. I keep folks from takin' stuff off of the old *Killdeer* too. Folks think because she's wrecked here, she's ripe for salvage. But I tell them that I'm crew and she ain't never been left abandoned."

"What happened to the cargo?"

"Well, Mr. Walker, the deck crew, Johnny and Pete, took it off the boat and they say that they'll deliver it to where we were takin' it. Heard that they borrowed a truck."

I remembered the two deckhands. They always seemed to be drunk, and I guessed that they would probably take the cargo and sell it. They were probably having a big party right now.

Jason interrupted my gloomy thoughts. "Now, here's the reason I brung y'all down here. Open that last boiler door, please Mr. Walker." He sat back in his chair, a sly grin on his face.

I swung the door open. It made an awful screeching noise. Black coal dust and ashes fell from its top and bottom.

"Well," said Jason. "What you see in there?"

I peered into the dark cavern and saw light glint off something shiny. I reached in and pulled out one of my old coffee sacks. Again, I felt into the darkness and dragged out the other one. "Jason! These are my bags!"

"I know. I saved 'em for you. If you'd told me what you were lookin' for I wouldn't have had to move that old stove." He pointed to a place above the coal pile. "They just fell right outta that space in the wall when she went on her side. I knew they was your's, so I kept 'em for you until I saw you again. And here you are."

"Did you open them?"

"Sure, I opened them, but I didn't take nothing out. It's all in there."

This is the man who once kicked me in the ribs and threatened to throw me into the boat's boiler. Now he was about my best friend, him and Wil.

God bless you, my friend," I said.

Jason looked down at the floor, embarrassed, "It weren't nothin', Mr. Walker."

I untied the string that held the piece of canvas top on the first sack and looked inside. The money was still crammed in there. The second sack had a piece of paper folded on top of the wads of bills. I took it out and recognized Capt. Hannah's handwriting.

"This is from the captain," I said to Jason. "How'd he know about my hidden bags?"

"Ah, man, everybody know about your sacks of money all along. But we all respects you and nobody touched it. The captain'd killed us!"

I read the note; *"To Dorky Walker, First Mate of the* Killdeer *and anyone else whom it may concern:*

Mr. Walker, I am in failing health and know that my days left on the river are few. I have no family, except that I consider you as a son. Because of your hard work, your intelligence, your desire, your ability to learn, and your natural-born common sense, I hereby give you ownership and command of the Killdeer, *all of her equipment, and stores along with all finances held at the Southern National Bank in Barriston. I have also notified Hampton J. Bradley, Esq., my attorney in Barriston, to prepare all the necessary paperwork to be ready when I go to be with the Lord.*

I have instructed the stoker, Jason, to put this letter in your secret coffee sacks alongside the stove. I also warned them that if they touched anything of yours I'd come back and skin their slimy carcasses with a dull knife.

May God bless you son. I'd ask you to consider keeping this crew we've had these past years. Take good care of them. They require discipline with a firm hand, but they are all good men.

Take good care of the Killdeer, *and be good to your crew.*

Signed:

Capt.Jonathan Hannah

Riverboat Killdeer."

Chapter Eight

The ways of the LORD are right;
the righteous walk in them,
but the rebellious stumble in them.

HOSEA 14:9

I felt like I might cry, and I didn't want to do that. I tried to say something, but only a squeak came out. Turning away, I muttered, "Thanks, Jason. Keepin' this bag for me means a lot."

"Y'know, Mr. Walker," said Jason. "This here ole boat ain't all that bad off." He waved his arms around the engine room. "Things have slid around and some of the bulkheads are messed-up, but these old boilers, and that engine, sho' got a lot mo' life in 'em!"

"You think she'd float again?"

"Why, I believe so. It'd just be a matter of rollin' her back onto her bottom and doin' some repairin."

I shook my head, thinking that it wouldn't be possible.

"No, Mr. Walker," Jason went on. "I looked over the bottom real good. She's got no big damage. Hull looks pretty tight, but if she sits long on this here sandbar, the sun'll dry her out and them old wood planks'll open-up like a cheap pocket comb."

"How we goin' get her a-floatin' again? She's 'way up on this snag," I said.

Leaning back against the dirty old boiler, Jason replied, "I saw them set a bigger boat than this right side-up once in New Orleans. I think we could do it—with a little help."

He said that we'd have to dig a couple of ditches under the boat and pull some heavy ropes over the top and through the ditches. Then we'd shovel-out a mess of sand from the closest-to-the-water side and pull on the ropes with a truck or a tractor, and roll her upright—right into the water!

I was excited about getting *Killdeer* working again, but I had one bad thought.

"Jason, I don't think I could pay for all that and the repairs too, with the money I got in these bags."

"Well, I wouldn't know about that. Captain Hannah always took care of things like that."

I remembered what the Captain's letter said; "*. . .along with all the finances held at the Southern National Bank in Barriston.*"

"Wil!" I yelled. "Let's get back to Pastor Mac's house, I think we got some travelin' to do!" We jumped down from the *Killdeer* and I yelled to Jason, "Don't let nobody take nothin' off our boat, Jason!" He gave me a big smile and nodded his head.

We ran like wild fire back to Pastor Mac's house and about scared Mrs. Gilley—I mean Mrs. MacAndrew—to death when we busted into the house all out of breath and dirty and sandy.

Pastor Mac was on his way home from Quickville. Wil and I went upstairs, stowed the bags of money under the bed, washed our faces and changed clothes. At the last minute, I opened the last bag and took out Captain Hannah's letter and a handful of money for our travel.

"Travelin' to where?" Pastor Mac had hardly gotten in the door when Wil and I started babbling about going to the bank in Barriston, and to see the attorney, Hampton J. Bradley. We told him what Jason said about saving *Killdeer* and the money in the bags, and how we had to try to get the riverboat back to work.

"I'll see if I can borrow Carl and Edward's truck and we can go tomorrow, bein' it's too late this day," he said. "That suit ye, my eager lads?"

It did!

Wil and I sat at the kitchen table planning how we'd get *Killdeer* rolled back upright, wondering how much money we'd have, and how much it would cost to get the boat back on the river. I hurt terribly and put my head down and fell asleep faster than a hungry hog chases a slop bug.

Suddenly, it was morning, and I was in the bed. I saw the door slowly open, a bushy head peeked in. It was Wil.

"Hey, 'Captain.' Time to get up and go see about getting you a riverboat!" he said.

"How'd I get here—in bed?"

"You sort-of walked, with help from Pastor Mac. Man, you were like a zombie!" He laughed and made like a monster.

I got dressed while Wil told me that Pastor Mac and he talked about the boat and Pastor Mac got excited about getting her back on her bottom. "I think you've got a new crewman now." said Wil.

The drive to Barriston was fun as we talked about *Killdeer* and the work ahead of us. Pastor Mac whispered to me, "We Scots always love a challenge, and with the good Lord's help, we'll have you a proper boat, Dorky!" We sure enough had a new man on *Killdeer's* crew.

After bouncing along the 25-miles of dirt road, I was hurting all over again, and thankful to be able to get out of the truck when we parked in front of the old red brick building where Hampton J.

Bradley had his office. Inside there was a funny looking little room, made out of metal wire and fancy screen. Pastor Mac said that it was a "lift" to take us up to the attorney's office. It shuddered and rattled and sort of swayed back and forth and Wil and I hung on with both hands as it raised us to the fourth floor. It was Wil and my first ride in a lift. We were glad when we finally got out.

Mr. Bradley was a short, round man, with a big mustache that bobbed up and down like a bird takin' off. He smiled a lot and his mustache made his grin look like it was as wide as his face, jowls and all. He sat at a big brown desk with a window behind him that I couldn't see anything except sky.

"Captain Hannah spoke well of you, young man," he said, a huge smile spreading across his face. "He left instructions for me to assign sole, legal ownership of the riverboat *Killdeer* to you upon his demise."

Pastor Mac leaned over to me and said, "That means when he dies."

"Oh," I said.

"The good captain left the accounting, inventory, expenditures, receipts, and budgeting in my hands, as well as payroll and investments," Mr. Bradley seemed to puff-up as he spoke, getting fatter by the moment. "I have handled his accounting for some eight years or so, to his total satisfaction. I tell you this with hopes that you'll continue to avail yourself of my services as you take over the riverboat business."

"If there is to be a 'riverboat business' after we right her off the sandbar and patch her up," said Pastor Mac. "The *Killdeer's* accounting will most likely stay in your hands, sir, if indeed there is any accounting to do."

I handed him the sheet that was in my money bag. "Captain Hannah said in his letter that there is a bank account in the Southern National Bank in Barriston. Do you know how much is in there?"

"Of course," said Mr. Bradley. "At the present time, there is a balance of $6,942, with an outstanding fuel bill of $126.97 to the Central Coal Company, and a deposit of $856.43 to be made for payment of the last cargo." He squinted at the ledger. "That will give you a $7,671.46 balance."

Wil and I bounced up and down in our seats and smiled like we just got away with something, when Pastor Mac said, "Well now, just how did the 'last cargo' get paid for when it went aground with the boat? I understand that the deckhands ran off with it."

Attorney Bradley leaned forward, his elbows on the desk, "The deckhands, Johnny and Pete, trucked the cargo to the dock at Millville and delivered it to the warehouse. They brought the bank draft to me. I paid them off. I will deposit that money Monday."

"May our dear God bless them rascals!" said Pastor Mac.

Bradley straightened-up. "There is also the matter of the investments Captain Hannah had my firm make over the years." He pulled another ledger from his desk. The drawer made a "screech" noise when he shoved it closed. "You will have control—after the ownership changes have been made—of a portfolio of various stocks and bonds, the value of which, at this present time, amounts to an additional $28,331.92. Your net value therefore is . . ." He mumbled something, doing figures on a separate piece of paper. ". . .a total of $35,274.05.

Pastor Mac smiled at us and said to Mr. Bradley, "How do we take care of the ownership changes, and when will they be effective?"

"Being made aware of the situation, and the loss of my dear friend, Capt. Hannah, I have the papers all ready for Mr. Walker's signature, so we can complete the legalities this day, sir."

"Let's be gettin' on with it then, we've a lot of work ahead of us," said Pastor Mac.

It took a long time for Mr. Bradley to explain each paper and for me to sign every one. I thought there must have been a thousand, but Mr. Bradley counted only 18. We talked awhile, Pastor Mac asking me hard questions about keeping Mr. Bradley doing the same job, and transferring money and stuff. Finally satisfied, Pastor Mac, Wil, and I shook Bradley's hand.

We all ate at a little restaurant next door, then headed the old Ford back down to Quickville, which was a lot better than riding in the "lift".

I suddenly felt like we were a family, something I'd never known before. Pastor Mac, Mrs. Mac, and Wil were a family now. I didn't feel like I didn't belong to that family, but I didn't feel like I was a part of it either. Jouncing along in the old truck, I had time to think about what I could do to have a family of my own someday. Work hard, save, stay close to the Lord and those that I love, and if I did that, I figured that someday, someone would come along for me, and there'd be a whole new family born. I fell asleep for a little while, and woke up as we rattled up to Pastor Mac's house.

Sitting around the dinner table, talking and joking, was for me about the best part of being a family. A lot of the talk was about *Killdeer* and how it was a good business and how I was very lucky to be blessed with the opportunity to get her back working.

The next morning, while Pastor Mac prepared for the next day's sermon, Wil and I went back to *Killdeer*, taking Jason a box of food, some clothes, a jacket and flashlight. Jason had not been sitting around.

The sand bar was stacked with things from the boat. "Makin' her lighter," he explained. He had a row of small tree limbs stuck in the sand along one side. "Gotta dig out the sand up to them sticks, then she'll roll right into the water bottom-side-down."

Jason got all quiet when we gave him the things we'd bought for him, and he turned away and rubbed at his face. Wil said that he was cryin'.

The next morning Wil and I went and got Jason to go to Kirkcaldy Church with us. He was ready, dressed in his new clothes and shiny shoes. First time I'd seen him without his raggedy old boots. He looked like a new man. He'd even shaved.

The new Kirkcaldy Christian Church was right nice looking with a new sign and a steeple with a bell in it so that Pastor Mac didn't have to call the faithful by shaking his little bell.

Pastor Mac met us at the door and gave Jason a hug, which embarrassed the old black man, but I could tell that he liked being accepted.

The church was a lot bigger than the old Kirkcaldy church on the hillside, and I could see that Mac and the people really had worked hard to make it nice. Mrs. MacAndrews waved and smiled at us. Wil went over to her and they talked for a few minutes until Pastor Mac went to the front. We found seats up close and listened to his sermon about a man named Job who got in a whole lot of trouble before God made things right for him. It was his faith in God that turned things around. I thought of how I had been ignoring my faith, and my light, and wondered how things would be for me now if I hadn't done that. I looked around at the new church and the crowd of folks inside. Pastor Mac had kept his faith, even after I wrecked his old church, and now he had a new life, a new wife, a new house, and a very fine church right down in town.

I had run away from Pastor Mac, and church, and my light, and look what happened: Capt. Hannah was dead and his *Killdeer* was laying on her side on a sand spit. I wondered if what happened to Pastor Mac's old church and the Bible's Job was the same thing. Both had big problems, but their faith in God fixed them. Maybe if I would have been more loyal to God and his words, I'd still be with Pastor Mac, or Capt. Hannah on the *Killdeer*.

As the sermon ended and Mrs. Douglas began playing a hymn on the piano, I wondered if there was any chance of me getting back on the good side of God.

Chapter Nine

But if we walk in the light, as he is in the light, we have fellowship with one another, and the blood of Jesus, his son, purifies us from all sin.

1 JOHN 1:7

It was drizzling a little rain Monday morning. The river was dark and almost still. None of the long-necked gray birds were poking around the shore, and the trees looked like bony, black, scary creatures rising out of the dead water. We found Jason already hard at work as we waded out to the snag. He was in his dirty old overalls and looked a lot like those trees. His face lit-up like a Halloween pumpkin when he saw us, and gave us a "How do!"

We were busy dragging chunks of the old Quickville pier off of the *Killdeer* when a horn honked. There, at the river's edge, was Carl and Edward's old truck filled with men and pipe and all sorts of equipment. Pastor Mac jumped down off the back and waved to us. All of the men went to work moving and dragging stuff over to the raft. Pastor Mac waded out to us grinning, "The men of the town and church had a meetin' Sunday night and decided that the old *Killdeer* here, is a menace to navigation, an eyesore, and needs to be put back to work on the river!"

I saw Johnny Smallhead dragging great coils of rope and even Mason Quick, camera swinging from his neck, dragging pipe across the sand. The man with crutches from the store was on top of the truck, handing down things to the others. Someone began to screw sections of pipe together, and Johnny Smallhead was tying a small rope to the end of one of the long pieces of pipe. A hose ran from a gasoline engine pump, and it was being connected to the pipe. Men went to work with shovels, scooping-out great loads of sand from where Jason had his markers stuck. Everything was going so fast, I couldn't keep up with it all.

Two holes were being dug alongside *Killdeer's* hull, and suddenly, the gas engine started with a roar. Two men began to poke the pipe into the side of the first hole before the second one was even finished. Water gushed out of the pipe and began to wash a hole in the sand under the boat. They kept pushing the pipe under until water gushed up on the other side. The men dug down to the end of the pipe and held the rope while other pulled the pipe back through the washed-out tunnel. That small rope was tied to one of the big ropes, and it was pulled under the boat's side. The same thing at the other hole, and soon there were two heavy ropes going all the way around *Killdeer's* hull.

There were new shovels for every man and every man began digging away the sand, first up close to *Killdeer*, then they started at the water's edge and dug as deep as they could until the water filled-in. The area in the center was left for last because, I was told, they could dig that out without fear of *Killdeer* falling or sliding down on top of men digging near the boat. Once the water filled in up close to the boat's bottom, the ropes could pull her upright, into the dug-out area. Once there, she would be afloat and could be towed from the sandbar snag.

I heard a loud chugging noise coming from shore, and saw the black exhaust smoke of a tractor as it edged its way through the trees. It neared the water's edge and the ropes were tied to it.

Mac was beside me. "It's God's work that brought all of these men, good and bad, together to help you, Dorky."

I nodded in silent agreement knowing that it was really their love and respect for Pastor Mac that did it.

Just before dark, the center section broke through to the river and filled with water in a few moments. Johnny Smallhead had the big pump running and was blasting the sand from the hole with the pressure from the hose. The lines to the tractor were tightened and its engine roared with power. *Killdeer* slid a little, then slowly rolled upright and collapsed the sand bank under it. She dropped easily into the water. An all-day job for just a few minutes of success. An enormous cheer went up from the men, and they were slapping each other on the back and punching their shoulders like they just won a football championship. Pumps were lifted aboard in case *Killdeer* started leaking.

A spotlight from a work barge lit up *Killdeer* as she was slowly towed away from her sandy prison.

That night, Mrs. MacAndrew laid out a big dinner for us. We went over what the cost would be for what we did today. It was $97 for the shovels, $25 for the use of the tractor. Everything else was loaned by the men. Mac suggested that we host a big lunch or dinner for them in thanks. We all agreed.

All of us working together like that made it seem like we were a real family. I imagined that I had a father, a mother, and even a brother. I knew it was just a dream, but it felt good to have such a dream.

The hills to the south of Quickville hid a slough that ran from the river into a narrow bay. At the end of the bay, a pier and a railway that was used to drag boats up out of the water stuck out from a tree-sheltered boat yard called Quickriver Boat Building Company.

The owner, Duke Farley, was a distant relative of the original owner, Silas Quick.

Wil and I walked through town, along a dirt road, rutted by the years of trucks running to and from the boat yard. We came out under the huge cypress trees, Irish moss hanging all over them like spaghetti, and magnolia trees that covered the boat yard like a roof. *Killdeer* was laying alongside the pier. One pump was spitting out spurts of water, and two men were sawing on pieces of wood. Most of the paddlewheel paddles were gone, and there were big holes in the side of the cargo area.

As we walked out on the pier, one man looked up and yelled, "You boys stay off this here pier. Go play somewhere else!" I yelled right back at him, "I'm Dorky Walker, and *Killdeer* is my boat. I held up Captain Hannah's note, and Attorney Bradley's letters.

"Aye, sorry, Mr. Walker," he said as we walked up. "Didn't know it was you." He was bent with age and his skin looked like it belonged on one of the alligators that lay around in the slough. "I'm Farley, Duke Farley. This here . . ." he pointed at a younger man still busy sawing wood. ". . .is my son, Malcomb."

"I'll be needin' to know what repairs are goin' to be needed here, Mr. Farley, and how much it's gonna cost."

The old man scratched his ear with the end of a pencil. "Pastor Mac already okayed startin' on the repairs to the wheelhouse and the paddle wheel. He has the estimate, and your man, Jason, is down below workin' like his pants are on fire."

We went aboard and heard a roaring noise from the engine room. "Sounds like somethin' runnin' down there," said Wil. I looked down the ladder and saw Jason, wearing only a pair of cut off pants washing down the whole place with a high pressure spray of water.

We waited in the wheelhouse, straightening up things in the chart table drawers and shoving boxes and chairs back where they belonged. When all the noise down below died down, we called out to Jason. He hurried up the ladder.

"Hullo Mr. Capt. Walker, and Willie, the old *Killdeer* here look pretty good, don't she?"

Jason had cleaned the whole engine room, furnaces and boilers. It looked better than I ever saw it before, it did. And I told him so. That brought a big, white-toothed smile to his sweaty face.

We spent the whole day putting things back together. The mast had been lost along with the towing and running lights, horn, and anchor light.

Mr. Farley took us out back to a big pile of old boat parts and showed us a mast. It was complete with all the lights. "This here came offen' a workboat that was used when they replaced the old railroad bridge. It was too tall, so we took it off and fitted a shorter one on the workboat for 'em," he said. "We'll let you have it for $40."

This would be my first decision as captain and owner of *Killdeer*. I needed to think hard about it.

We worked until dark that day, right alongside Jason. He made a sleeping area in the engine room. As we were leaving, I said, "Jason, how long has it been since you been paid?"

Smiling wide, he said, "Capt. Walker, y'all have already paid me when you brought me that box of vittles and clothes and things. I sure don't need anything more than what I got here. You don't worry yourself about me, I'm fine. And I sure thank you for that."

That night I told Pastor Mac that I wanted to give Farley $40 for the mast and lights. I told him, "He said he'd put it up for us for nothin."

"That sounds like a sure fair price, lad, and Farley's as honest as any man walkin' around, he is."

So there it was. I'd made my first commitment to buy something for the boat, and for the first time felt like I was really the captain of the working riverboat, *Killdeer*.

The work went quickly. Pastor Mac spent long hours repairing the cabin, cargo hold, deckhouse and all the other woodworking doings she needed. Turns out that Wil was a real good painter. Best of all, he enjoyed doing it. He started way up on the new mast, worked his way down to the cabin top, did the sides of the wheelhouse, and as soon as Mac finished a repair, Wil would get it primed and painted straight-away. It was only a week in the boatyard that *Killdeer* looked better than she ever had.

When she was all finished, We had a big Saturday night party right there on the Quickriver Boat Building Company's dock. All those who had helped us were there. Mrs. MacAndrew and the other women made a wonderful bunch of food and drink. Mason Quick brought some banjo and guitar players, and the music went on into the night. Everybody was surprised at how good the old riverboat looked. Jason had the engine working just right, and put up some steam just so he could blow the whistle.

Wil came up to me in the dark and whispered, "Dor, don't look, but there's a couple of men standin' over there by the boathouse in the dark." It was hard to keep from looking. We walked around behind a boat lying upside-down and peeked at the figures in the shadows.

"What you suppose they want?"

"I don't know, Wil, but I'll get Pastor Mac, and we'll go around the buildin' behind 'em and find out, or chase 'em off."

"Or get stabbed or shot," said Wil.

I wandered over to Pastor Mac, told him what Wil had told me, and we strolled around the front of the old boathouse until we were out of sight, then hurried around the building.

The two men were standing in the shadows. They didn't look much bigger than me, and Pastor Mac was way bigger. We sneaked up behind them. Both of us had picked-up pieces of wood to use if need be.

Mac roared, "What'll be ye hidin' out here for, lads?" The men leaped straight up, turned, and both of them looked like they'd come face to face with a hungry alligator.

It was Johnny and Pete, the *Killdeer's* old crew, just watching the doings. They were shaking like a willow in a hurricane, sputtering and mumbling. I told Mac who they were, and we dragged them, still shaking, over to join the party.

Johnny explained, "We was headin' downriver to New Orleans when we heard that the old *Killdeer* was being repaired, so we came a-lookin."

"Didn't want to bust in on your doin's," added Pete.

"Oh, me dear, dear lads!" howled Mac, "'Tis you two who will make this a real joyous celebration, it will!" He threw his arms around them and led them off toward the food.

A bit later, Pastor Mac came over to Wil and me. "Those boys are going to New Orleans lookin' for work. I think that we owe them their old jobs back on your boat, boy. What are ye thinkin' about that?"

"But we don't even have any haulin' to do yet," I said.

"That'll come, that'll come. I think we owe these two a lot for their honesty in takin' that old cargo to it's rightful place, don't ye?"

"How about we tell them to see what they can do in New Orleans," I suggested, "and that we'll have work for them on *Killdeer* if'n they don't find nothin' down there."

"Aye, good thinkin' lad. I'll tell them." Pastor Mac headed over to the pier where the two men were standing looking at the boat, chomping on sandwiches.

That night, Pastor Mac and I went over the cost of everything and found that we had enough left over, without getting into the invested money, to start *Killdeer* working again, pay Jason, and even Johnny and Pete, while we got the boat a cargo or two.

I washed-up and climbed into the bed, but couldn't go to sleep. The excitement of the day, the thoughts of what would come tomorrow, and in the future, had my mind running like a flooding river heading into the unknown. I was on my way to really being somebody. somebody other than "that Dorky kid."

Chapter Ten

For God, who said, "Let light shine out of darkness,"
made his light shine in our hearts to give us the light of the
knowledge of God's glory displayed in the face of Christ.

2 CORINTHIANS 4:6

The room was dark. The house was quiet. I lay there staring at nothing and thinking of everything. I finally closed my eyes, and there, like a far-off river beacon, was my light. It reminded me to say my nightly prayer and to ask God for direction and courage for my new venture as a riverboat captain.

"God, this here's Dorky. I want thank you for bringin' the whole town together to get old *Killdeer* back to work. And thank you for bringin' Johnny and Pete back too." The light shone steadily, so I added, "Lord, I know I've been away from you lately, and I know that you will never leave me or forsake me, but I guess I sort of did that to you. I guess what I want to know is, will you forgive me for that?"

The light went off. I think my heart stopped until it came back on, a little brighter too, it seemed. I let my breath out in relief. "Thank you, Lord."

"I guess I'm learnin', Father, that Your ways aren't like our ways. When I have asked for somethin', you've pretty much always done it, but man, you got scary ways. I still don't understand why Capt. Hannah had to die, and why *Killdeer* had to be wrecked." The light stayed steady like a bright little planet in a vast, dark universe. "But

95

thank you, God, for bringin' me back to Pastor Mac, and this here town."

As I was ending my prayer, a thought came to me; I had come along to remind Capt.Hannah of his time with Pastor Mac, and that helped to bring him back to the Bible, just in time, before he died. If I hadn't come to *Killdeer*, he still would have died, but wouldn't be close to the Lord. He wouldn't have someone to take over the riverboat for him. The ideas kept coming to me, as if someone was telling me things.

I guess the boat was wrecked so that the town would come together with Pastor Mac and be like a big family, held together by Mac and the church. It sure had done that, alright. A peaceful feeling sort of swelled-up inside me, and I said to my light, "Oh, I get it now, Lord. Thanks. Oh, and, Amen, Father." It blinked off then on again, and I was asleep in a half-second.

In the morning, Pastor Mac and I stopped at the City Hall, a room in the back of the hardware store, and made arrangements to tie *Killdeer* up in the slough where an old dock stuck out from the shore. It would be a perfect place to load cargo and keep the riverboat out of the fast running river.

Killdeer looked mighty fine, sitting at the boatyard dock, all painted nice and shiny. Jason was cleaning the wheelhouse windows as we went aboard. "Morn'n Capt. Walker. And to you too Rev. MacAndrew," he said. "Mr. Farley told me to tell y'all to come to the boatshop when y'all has the time."

The boatyard's shop was a barn-like building with big doors at both ends. A railroad track ran all the way through it and down a ramp into the water. Boats could be launched right out of the shop. It was dim inside. The only light came from rows of long windows up in the center of the roof and age cracks scatted around the windows.

Wispy, faint clouds of dust and sawdust were illuminated in shafts of dim sunlight. They angled down through the still air from cracks and breaks in the old wood siding. Duke Farley sat at a desk made from a sheet of heavy plywood atop two wooden sawhorses. Sawdust covered papers, tools and boat parts that lay among the books. A coffee can filled with pencils and pens sat near the edge, about to fall off. His chair was a wooden shipping crate. It reminded me of Capt. Hannah's desk aboard *Killdeer*. He stood up and shook hands with Pastor Mac, then me. I tried to push the can of pencils and pens farther onto the desk and discovered that it was screwed down.

Half an hour later we left with the boatyard's bill all paid, and happy with the charges. Pastor Mac took out a folded paper and a pencil and did some figuring. "'pears you still have about $5,023.05 in operatin' capital left," he said.

"That's a lot of money!" I said.

"Aye, but ye'll be usin' that up pretty fast when the boat goes back to work. Ye'll have fuel bills, wages, dockin' fees, insurance, food, and everyday expenses whist ye are away from here."

"*WE* will," I said.

"What say you, boy?"

"I said, '*WE* will have a lot of expenses.' You're part of the crew now, Mac, and you'll share in the profits when they start comin' in."

"That's mighty generous of you lad, but I'll not be floatin' off down the river every time you—*we*—get a load to carry."

"No sir. You've already done your part. Without you getting the men together and helping to get her back afloat and workin', she'd still be lyin' on her side out there in the river." He stared off at some distant point.

"I'm goin' to be livin' on board," I said. "Me and Jason, and usin' Quickville as our . . . what do you call it? Our 'home port'?"

Mac turned away and wiped the back of his hand across his eyes. "Aye, well then, lad, it's proud I am to be a part of your crew." He blew his nose and wiped at his eyes again. I thought that he might be crying a little, but I didn't say anything.

Two nights later, Pastor Mac got a phone call from Attorney Bradley saying that a previous customer, Marshall Machine of Barriston, needed a bid on hauling a 600-pound lathe to Lewisport, Indiana. Mac dug into *Killdeer's* invoice books and log book and started looking for what Captain Hannah charged for that kind of weight and distance in the past.

"Ah, very well, lad," he finally said. "It appears that Captain Hannah did similar trips like that. I'll call Mr. Bradley in the morning with the price, if you approve, Dorky."

"Sure." I struggled to remember how long it took us to make it to Barriston before. "Tell them we can be there in three days—I hope."

Pastor Mac had a long talk with Hampton J. Bradley and was happy to hear that the attorney would act as an agent for *Killdeer*. He would notify all the past customers of the new ownership, and solicit new customers. The scheduling of pick-up and deliveries, and prices would be up to us.

I rushed to the boat the next morning.

"Jason! Jason! We got our first job! Let's get ready to make a pick-up in Barriston, and take it to Lewisport, right away!"

"We goin' maybe need one mo' hand onboard, Mr. Walker," said Jason.

"Wil is on his way, and last night my light said we'd have more help," I blurted that out forgetting that Jason knew nothing about the light in me.

"Your *whaaat*?" he squealed.

"Ah, man, I'll tell you about it later, okay? Right now we need to get ready to go."

Jason went below mumbling, "He don't know what he's talkin' about . . . a *light*? What kinda light? Lordy!"

I laid-out the river charts and took a pencil from the old tin can where Captain Hannah kept them. I looked at the pencil, short and all worn-down by the Captain's hand. I thought of him, and tears started to come, and I realized how much I loved that gruff old man. I thought of Pastor Mac, and how hard it was going to be if he too went to be with the Lord.

The boat rocked and I heard someone coming aboard. It was Wil, both arms filled with bags. "Whatcha got there, Buddy?" I asked.

"Well, it seems our new captain forgot all about feedin' us poor crewmen, so Mrs. MacAndrew made us some grub for the trip." Wil grinned at me and headed for the galley.

"That kinda talk'll be what we call 'mutiny' Mr. Gilley!" Then I thought that Wil should be the First Mate, even though he had no experience, but he did learn fast and had been willing to do any and all things for the boat—and me.

Jason had steam built-up and I checked the steering, compass, radio and lights, so there was no reason not to get underway. "Cast-off the dockline, Wil," I yelled out the wheelhouse door. "We're headin' for Barriston!"

"Aye, Captain Dor," he replied with a pirate's growl to his voice.

I levered-up the throttle handle and *Killdeer* slid away from the dock, pointing her blunt nose toward the opening to the river.

There was a sudden jolt, and a crashing noise and *Killdeer* stopped dead in the water. I jumped down the ladder and headed for the stern, wondering what had happened. Wil was working with all his strength to push the rear of the boat away from the old pier.

"I thought we were clear of that!" I yelled.

"No, man," he grunted. "You swung out too soon and the stern hit this old post here."

"*Piling*," I said.

Wil glanced at me, "What?"

"Well, that's not a post, Wil, it's a piling," I explained.

"Yeah well, whatever it is, you plum run into it. We're stuck here now!"

Just then Jason came on deck. "Whatcha all doin' out here?"

I explained that I swung the stern too soon and hit the pier.

"Didn't ya know, boy, that boats steer from the rear end?" Grinning, he wrapped his big arms around the piling and pulled the boat back away as easy as if he was pulling a hog from a bog. "Y'all better get back to the wheelhouse, captain, we is free now!"

All I could think to say was, "Thanks Jason."

I gave two short warning blasts of the whistle as *Killdeer* moved smoothly from the slough. Still shaking a bit from hitting the pier, I spun the wheel and headed her upstream toward Barriston.

Wil was on the foredeck coiling-up our dock lines when he suddenly turned, waved his arms at me, and pointed toward shore. There, on what was left of the Quickville dock, stood Johnny and Pete, waving us over. I swung *Killdeer* close, and they jumped aboard, laughing and clapping their hands.

"We decided to go to New Orleans after this here trip. If you'd been a couple of minutes earlier," said Johnny, "We'd missed you!"

Free and clear on the river with no other boat traffic around us, I took a moment to close my eyes. The light shone brightly. "Well, Lord," I said softly, "I'm learnin' how you do things. I guess I snagged that old dock to give Johnny and Pete time to get to the Quickville pier. Now, I ain't sayin' you have only one way of doing things, but from now on, I won't be afraid or worried when bad things happen, 'cause I know you're doing all things for good. Even if I don't understand how or why."

The light blinked off and on, and I was calmed by peace and renewed confidence.

On the run upriver to Barriston, I showed Wil what to do while he would be steering *Killdeer*. He took to it right handy, and I was sure he'd be an able helmsman without much work from me.

I took the helm as darkness slowly pushed the daylight to the west and the river became like a black asphalt road. On both sides, the trees are slowly waving sentinals guiding us through the darkness. I love the quiet of the river at night, only the boat's noises and the occasional horn or whistle of a passing river craft, often unseen.

I heard the call of a Killdeer bird.

The next morning we docked at Barriston in a drizzling rain. Dark clouds hovered low over the town and it was as quiet as a graveyard. Only the occasional sound of a riverboat whistle sliced through the gloom. Leaving Jason and the two deckhands aboard, Wil and I went to the Dockmaster's office at the far end of the pier. It took about 15 minutes to do the paperwork and for him to give us our manifest papers for the machinery.

Back at *Killdeer*, we saw Jason and the two crewmen sitting on a bench by the warehouse building.

"Lookit there, Cap'n," said Jason, pointing to the boat.

There was a big chain looped around the dock's bollard and through *Killdeer's* paddle wheel. A yellow piece of paper was taped to the side of the cabin.

"Notice of Violation And Quarantine Status" it said. I read the form with the boat and my name penciled in on it. Our papers were not in order and the boat would be held until they were. Violations were; expired registration and unlicensed operator. We were not even allowed on board until the violations were corrected.

I was stunned. We were being put out of business before we got our first job loaded! I gave Jason, Johnny, and Pete enough of the money I had left for them to spend the day in town and eat lunch, and Wil and I headed for Hampton J. Bradley's office.

"Bull feathers!" roared the attorney. "As far as the River Authority knows, Capt. Hannah is still the master of record on *Killdeer*, and we have a temporary registration on file to cover the boat while she was out of commission at the boatyard in Quickville!" His mustache bounced up and down like the wake of a passing boat was hitting it. He gathered-up some papers from a filing cabinet and said, "I'll get this corrected at the River Authority. You boys go on back to your boat and I'll meet you there."

It was afternoon and the drizzle had stopped. The skies were still gray and rumpled. Attorney Bradley came striding down the dock with two men hurrying alongside him. One was a small bald man wearing a black suit, the other a big man who could easily be mistaken for a boxer or a wrestler. He was dressed in work clothes.

"As it stands," started Bradley, "The River Authority knows of Capt. Hannah's death and you, unfortunately, are not licensed to operate on the river without a Master's Certificate—in effect—a license." He introduced the smaller man, "This is Albert Fitzsimmons of the River Authority. He can release the boat for this trip under the Temporary Registration, but you cannot be her master."

"How can I get licensed?" I asked.

Mr. Fitzsimmons responded, "You have a sufficient number of days on the river as first mate under Captain Hannah to qualify to take the Master's Examination. I have brought you a study guide. If you prepare for the exam, we can give it to you on your return trip here. But you'll need to study hard—the exam is not easy!"

Bradley took the other man's arm, "This is Capt. Harvey Harlin." The big man nodded at us, but stayed silent. "He will command *Killdeer* on this trip, and until you pass the examination and are duly licensed to take over." He lowered his voice and bent his head toward me, "I know that you are qualified and able to be her master, but we have to follow the law, understand?"

Captain Harlin immediately took charge, got the cargo loaded and talked to the crew about what he expected of each of them. We left Barriston that evening, heading for Lewisport. I hunkered-down under the galley table on my old sleeping pad and began to study the book that Mr. Fitzsimmons gave me. It felt odd not being at the wheel, and I listened to every sound and felt every movement of the riverboat as it labored upstream. Whenever Captain Harlin blew the whistle, I jumped in surprise.

I came to realize that most of what I was reading in the book I already knew. Capt. Hannah had been putting it into my head all during those long hours of navigating the river. He taught me all the while, and I didn't even know it!

I hadn't slept since we left Quickville and was struggling to stay awake while lying there studying for the test. The movements and sounds of *Killdeer* making way soon edged consciousness aside and I fell hard asleep.

Chapter Eleven

Be strong and courageous.
Do not be afraid or discouraged.

1 CHRONICLES 22:13

"Y ou're not goin' get your Master's ticket sleepin' all day Mr. Walker!" Capt. Harlin was standing over me. It was morning. I had slept all night. The lantern hanging under the table for me to see by was out of fuel. I stumbled out, dragging the guide book and the lantern. "Sorry Mr. Harlin," I mumbled.

"Mr. Wil told me you'd been up all the night before, so I let you sleep. Can't pass a license test if you can't stay awake."

I washed the sleep out of my eyes and looked for the others.

We were alongside the Lewisport pier, and men were loading the machinery onto a big trailer truck. Wil was sweeping out the cargo deck.

I yelled, "Hey, Wil, where's Johnny and Pete?".

"Hey! Hi Dor!" Wil propped the broom against the side of the boat. "Glad you got some sleep, man. You were starting to look like a hoot owl, big old weird eyes!" He made a face with bug eyes.

"The guys went into town to find Lewisport Shipping. They've got a small cargo for us to take to Quickville. Something for Mr. Quick's newspaper."

"Why don't Lewisport Shippin' carry it?"

"The agent said it was too small for them to run one of their big paddle wheelers down there. Since we're going that way, it's our job!"

Just then a big truck rolled up alongside *Killdeer* with Johnny and Pete waving from atop it. "How'd we get this job?" I asked Johnny.

"Mr. Bradley called around looking for loads for us and found this one," he said.

Four crates were unloaded and moved aboard. *Killdeer* left the Lewisport dock just before sunset. Captain Harlin called me to the wheelhouse. He had the study guide in his hand. "Sit down and let's see if you can answer any of these questions." I sat.

For the next four hours, he asked me question after question, sometimes correcting me, and then asking the same one again later. I was getting most answers pretty close to right, and learning a lot at the same time. It was hard for him to read in the dim light, and he couldn't have a bright light because he wouldn't be able to see the river ahead through the front window glass. I think he was making-up a lot of the questions from what he knows. But that didn't matter, it was still all good stuff to learn.

I made us coffee and we ate the last of Mrs. MacAndrew's bag of food.

I took the helm while he took a break. It was good to be back behind the big wheel. The river was a bright, curving road ahead, lit up by the harvest moon. Ducks scudded out of our way, flapping and squawking their annoyance. It was a beautiful night on the river, one to make a man want to do this for his whole life.

Capt. Harlin returned and said, "You better go get some sleep so you'll be ready for that test tomorrow."

"Do you think I'll pass it?"

"Well, Capt. Hannah taught you well. You surprised me." He handed me the study guide. "I think you'll do okay."

In bed, I figured that my light would tell me if I was going to do well like Capt. Harlin said. I said a prayer, thanking God for our safe passage, getting the two cargos and asked that he bless our crew and Capt. Harlin too. I kept my eyes closed, expecting to see my light, but the darkness was just darkness. I opened my eyes and scooched down to get more comfortable, and again looked for my light.

It wasn't there.

That worried me, but I figured that maybe I was just too tired to talk with my light this night. I woke up twice during the night looking for my light. It still was not there.

In the morning we were nearing Barriston and I looked to my light again. Not there. I began to worry that I'd done something to lose the light. I couldn't think of a thing.

There was no loading or unloading to do at the Barriston dock, so Johnny and Pete went into town, and Jason left to visit friends. Capt. Harlin slept.

Attorney Bradley came to take me to the examination for my riverboat license. He had a new, shiny four-door car and I felt pretty important riding to the test in it. The building was at the river's edge. A low, long, gray wooden boxy-looking place with small windows high up on its side. It reminded me of a prison I once saw.

As we pulled up, I closed my eyes and eagerly looked for my light. Nothing. I felt bad, rejected. Then I remembered God's words; *Never will I leave you. Never will I forsake you.* I guessed that he just had more important business than me right then.

The test took four hours. It was hard, and used a lot of words I'd never heard before. Even though I tried my hardest, I didn't know if I passed or not.

I waited by the river's edge for Attorney Bradley to come get me. I closed my eyes twice, looking for my light. It didn't show.

Capt. Harlin was waiting and ready to take *Killdeer* on down the river to Quickville. Johnny and Pete had not come back, and he had searched all the taverns in town. We had to leave without them.

Wil asked me a million questions about the test, and kept saying, "You passed it. Yup, I know you passed it!" I wasn't so sure.

We tied up at Quickville the next night and slept aboard the boat. In the morning the three of us managed to unload the four crates for Mr. Quick. That's when Capt. Harlin shook Wil's and my hands and said, "I've enjoyed running with you men, and I'll see you when your next trip is scheduled." He slapped me on the back, "Don't you worry none about that test, Mr. Walker. You'll do okay." He walked down the road, his sea bag over his shoulder.

Two weeks later I was invited to have dinner with Pastor Mac and Mrs. Mac, and Wil. They had chicken and mashed potatoes and pie and ice cream after.

We sat on the front porch after dinner and watched the moon creep up from behind the mangroves. A flock of geese flew over, slow and graceful, passing their V-formation in front of the shimmering moon. It was beautiful and I thought how lucky we all were to live in such a fine place. Then things started changing.

Pastor Mac leaned back in the porch swing and said, "Wil, I have some wonderful news for you, lad!"

Wil straightened up, "About the school?"

"Yes, you have been accepted, and ye have to be there next Monday." This was Thursday.

Pastor Mac explained, "Wil is going to be going to Christ First Theological College in Atlanta, Georgia." He'll someday take over Kirkcaldy Christian Church—he'll be 'Pastor Wil', he will!"

"Wow, Wil!" I said, then thought it sounded foolish. "I didn't even know you were lookin' to do anythin' like that."

"I've been studying for a long, long time, and Pastor Mac's been helping me a lot. He was afraid that I'd change my mind about being a preacher after I went to work on *Killdeer*, but I still want to do it, badly. It's been hard to find a school that'd take me, Dor." He looked happy. "I don't have a very good—what they call 'formal education.'"

"Aye, he's been studyin' hard though, he has," said Pastor Mac. "I'm proud of the lad!"

"Me too," I said. "But who'll take over on *Killdeer* when you're gone?

"Well, lad," Mac put his hand on my shoulder. "There's lots of able men around who'd love to work with you on the riverboat. We'll be findin' someone, sure."

Wil was going to have to take the train that Saturday. He had a lot to do, and I might not see him before he left, so we said our goodbyes right then. "You always got a place on *Killdeer*, pal," I said.

"I'll write you a letter once in awhile to let you know how I'm doin', okay?"

I left them and walked back to the boat, finding Jason sitting on a suitcase on the dock. "Jason, what's the suitcase for?"

"Ah, Mr. Walker, I gotta go home to my mama. She's powerful sick, and nobody there to take care of her." There were tear trails running down his cheeks through the coal dust.

"Man, that's tough. Do you need some money to get you home?"

"No, sir. I still got all my pay from a long time." He patted his overall's pocket. "I sure hate to leave you and this here boat, Mr. Walker, but I gotta go take care of my mama. She really old!"

"Sure. Good luck." I felt sorry for him and shook his hand. He walked stoop-shouldered through the trees toward the south. "You come back whenever you can, hear?" He waved, then stopped, and came hurrying back. I thought he must have changed his mind.

"I almost forgot Captain Walker. Here's a letter for you."

I slipped the letter from its yellow envelope. It was a telegram from the River Authority.

"Dear Mr. Dorky Walker,

I regret to inform you that your score on the Riverboat Master's examination did not meet our standards for the captaincy for which you applied. Your score total of 79% is six percentage points less than needed for successful completion of the examination.

The exam may be taken again after a three-month waiting period from the first examination date.

Contact the River Authority to reschedule your examination."

Jason was gone, and *Killdeer* lay as quiet as a tomb. I went up to the wheelhouse and looked out over her bow. A big, yellow moon sent wavy paths of light shimmering across the water toward *Killdeer* like eels on the attack, and tree roots curling up from the bank looked like giant spider's legs. It was suddenly spooky on the boat, and for the first time since Pastor Mac pulled me from the flood waters, I was totally alone-no Captain, no crew, no Wil, and I never imagined that Jason would ever leave. I wanted to run away too, but knew that I couldn't. And I wanted to cry, but discovered that I'd outgrown that somewhere along that old river.

Afraid to close my eyes for fear that my light would not be there, I drank coffee and nibbled on an old wrinkled apple.

I crawled into the bunk under the foredeck that was Captain Hannah's cabin. It was the first time I'd been in there. I laid with my clothes still on, staring at the moonlight coming through a small overhead hatch.

I realized that everything was suddenly changed. I had *Killdeer*, but couldn't run her. I had failed the Master's Examination. What had I done for all this to happen to me all of a sudden? I couldn't figure it out or understand it. All I knew was that now I was alone. Totally and completely alone. I was afraid to close my eyes. I had been alone before, and it never much bothered me. My light came along and changed that. It was proof that there was someone there for me—always. Someone to talk to and who would answer me. My Father. The father I had never had before.

I don't remember falling asleep. I didn't dream, and I rolled and turned and kept waking up for a short time. Morning came suddenly, and I was still tired. And my light was not there for me.

I said a morning prayer as Pastor Mac taught me, but I didn't feel good about it. It was like talking to someone who had left the room.

My coffee woke me up and I went to work cleaning up the mess left over from the Lewisport trip. I found some of Wil's things in the corner of the cargo room where he slept and put them in a bag. Jason's last meal's plate and cup were in the engine room, and I could see his fingerprints in the coal dust. I missed his big voice and smiling face. I found two empty whiskey bottles and a girlie magazine left by Johnny and Pete. I sat down at Captain Hannah's old crate desk, my face in my hands and looked for the light. "Lord are you there? Are you with me? I feel awful lonesome, Father." The creaking of the old boat and rippling of water against her hull was all I heard. The blackness was untouched by light. I was surely alone.

When the sun reached the tops of the mangrove trees, I left *Killdeer* and wandered into Quickville. It was an early Friday morning and the town was just coming alive. Shops were opening up and sidewalks swept of the night's debris.

Kirkcaldy Church's door was closed, but unlocked. Inside, dim light filtered through the new colored windows, falling across the seats. A stand with four candles stood alongside the pulpit. I sat in my usual place and prayed. I didn't think that I could change God's mind about my light, but I needed to see if I could somehow understand why almost everything had suddenly been taken from me.

Minutes later, Pastor Mac came in the side door, humming a tune. He turned off the candle stand. He knelt on the step to the altar and prayed quietly. He rose, began to straighten-up the hymnals and Bibles on the seats, and saw me.

"Ah! My young friend, Capt. Walker!" He came and sat next to me. "Talkin' to the Lord, are ye?"

"Yessir. But I'm not a 'Captain' or anythin' else. I got the results of my test and I failed."

"Oh, me boy! Sorry to hear that, lad. Well then, you just study more, take it again, and surely you'll do it well and good next time."

"It's not only that, Mac." I told him of Jason, Johnny and Pete, and Wil, and even Captain Harlin, all up and leaving me all at the same time. With messing up on the exam, it was just too much at once. "Sure, I have *Killdeer*, but I can't even take her from the dock."

He nodded, "Aye, me boy, you're certainly goin' through a bad time, but you're surely handlin' it the right way, comin' here and prayin'. Prayer will get you through the toughest of situations, y'know."

"You know my light?"

"Ah, yes, your light! Ye are surely a blessed man, ye are."

"It's gone too."

Mac was quiet for a moment. He said, "Y'know lad, that light as you've described it, is like your earthly father—I understand—a father that ye never really had. But the Bible tells us that we must eventually leave our mother and father. And yet, the Holy Spirit will still be with you." He tapped his chest with a forefinger. "John said in John 8:12, *Jesus is the light of the world. He tells us that if we follow Him, we will never walk alone in the darkness, but will always have the light of life.*"

"But I don't know what to do, or how I'll ever get through all this."

Mac lowered his voice, "Well m'boy, James tells us. *'Blessed is the one who perseveres under trial because, having stood the test, that person will receive the crown of life that the Lord has promised those who love Him.'* Do you love Him, lad?"

"Sure I do, Mac. You taught me that."

"Very well then," he stood up. "Get on with your life! Things will turn-around for ye, lad. To be sure."

I felt better and went back to *Killdeer*. Working on the boat would take my mind off my troubles.

The starboard paddlewheel mounting was slightly damaged where I had snagged it on the piling before the Lewisport trip, so I went to work repairing it.

By the afternoon, I had finished the jobs I started, and sat in the wheelhouse studying for my next examination.

The sun sagged below the thick tangle of trees on the other bank of the slough. I lit the lantern and continued my study. When it got really dark, I fixed myself two sandwiches and went out on deck.

I heard the call of a Killdeer bird.

River frogs were battling shore side crickets for the loudest of the noise making, and in the windless night the trees listened quietly.

The water of the slough was an unrumpled inky black. Loneliness crept up on me in the darkness and pushed these sounds aside on its way into my consciousness. That sinister feeling of despair returned. Peace and hope fled.

The sounds of the night fell quiet as two men stumbled into view. I recognized one because of the crutches he struggled with. From their voices and their movements, I could see they were pretty drunk. They reminded me of Johnny and Pete on those *Killdeer* trips upriver. As their nearing voices grew louder, I could tell that they were arguing about something. They went past the boatyard down the path and into the woods.

The night critters started up, then fell silent again as one of the men returned, stumbling past the boatyard and into the woods from where the two of them had come.

I went into the woods where they had staggered. It was eerily quiet and so dark I could barely make my way along the narrow path. The trees opened up onto a clearing where a strange looking barrel with pipes and coils of tubing sticking out of it. Suddenly, I recognized that it was a still for making whiskey. A glass jar of a clear liquid was spilled onto the dirt. I saw a leg sticking out from behind the contraption.

I recognized the man lying there as one of the card players from the store. A crutch lay alongside him. I saw the other crutch sticking out of the bushes. I couldn't feel any pulse. I thought he must be dead.

A bright light suddenly flooded the clearing and a loud voice startled me, "Don't move, fella!" I recognized Sheriff Sardino's voice. "Keep your hands where I can see them. Back up toward me, slow-like." Two men grabbed my arms and dragged me to the middle of the clearing. They slammed on handcuffs.

"Sheriff, I saw these two men . . ."

"Quiet, boy!" He shined the light in my eyes. "I'm surprised it's you, Dorky. I thought Pastor Mac pretty much had you under control. Now I see that you're not only runnin' an illegal still out here, but it looks like you been busy beatin' on folks."

The two deputies dragged the body out into the light. "This here one's dead as a door knob."

"Pheweee, young fella, you in a mess 'o trouble here!"

The sheriff radioed for the coroner and the deputies took me to the patrol car hidden in the trees. One deputy stayed behind while the sheriff drove me to town.

"I was on the *Killdeer* . . ." I started.

"I like you Dorky, so for your own good, don't you say nothin' til we get you booked." Sheriff Sardino was a big man, and his voice thundered out of him like a volcano.

"We been watchin' this little whiskey operation there for a couple weeks now, figurin' you'd show up sooner or later."

"I didn't show up, I was just lookin' . . ."

"I told you to be quiet. Now if you don't understand that, I'd be just as happy to gag you, or maybe just thump you one on the head like you did old Melvin back there."

I wanted to tell him what happened, but I didn't want to get thumped on the head, so I stayed quiet all the way to the jailhouse.

The jail was a brick building and smelled of sweat and dirty socks. Dingy light from the hall made it even gloomier. The cell had a toilet with a metal seat and no lid, and a bed made of iron with a row of springs holding a wire grillwork. The mattress was dirty and lumpy. It was the source of the smell.

I was charged with what the sheriff called 'homicide' and 'illegal distilling' and some other terms that I didn't understand. I said nothing until the cell door slammed shut. "I didn't do nothin' Sheriff, and that's not my stuff out there, honest!"

"We'll see." He closed the office door, shutting me out.

The deputy who drove us there came in and stuffed a blanket between the bars. "Sleep tight." He said, grinning.

I put the blanket on the bed and lay down on top of it. I don't think I'd ever been so tired before, even after being up two days and all night running *Killdeer* on the river. I kicked-off my shoes and laid back on the meager mattress.

"Lord," I prayed aloud, "I just don't understand why everythin' is goin' wrong. What'd I do, Father, to have all this bad stuff come down on me like this?" I closed my eyes and slept a dreamless sleep.

Chapter Twelve

**And the God of all grace, who called you to his eternal glory
in Christ, after you have suffered a little while,
will himself restore you and make you strong,
firm and steadfast.**

1 Peter 5: 10

I didn't know where I was. I heard the rain on the roof and felt the cold before I opened my eyes from a night of restless sleep. I saw the gray sky and the falling rain through the bars of the cell window. I remembered the trouble that had come upon me. It was all a mistake, I reasoned, and after they let me tell what happened, they'll let me go. I prayed for that.

I wrapped myself in the ragged blanket and sat shivering, not so much from the cold as from icy fear that grabbed and shook me.

I could hear noises and voices in the jail office. After a long time, the door swung open, banging against the wall, and the deputy brought me a tray of food balanced on one hand and a cup in the other. "Here's some breakfast, fella." He looked like he'd been up all night. "Just shove the tray under the door when you're done." He handed it through an opening in the bars and left.

After I ate, I lay back on the bed and fell asleep. That terrible dream came back. The spider was on top of the spring again, and I prayed it wouldn't start bouncing, but it did. The black, hairy, creature came closer and closer with each bounce. I tried to figure out a way to escape or some way to stop the dream, but I had no ideas. I hunkered down in fear, unable to stop the beast or look away. Closer and closer it came, until I finally screamed and jerked upright, awake and sweating.

The door came open and Sheriff Sardino stomped in. "Whatsa matter with you, boy?"

"Sorry sheriff. I just had a bad dream."

"Well, cut it out!" He left, slamming the door behind him.

The time went slowly as I just sat there with nothing to do. I wished that I had another cup of coffee, but maybe Unkie had been right. It wasn't good for me. But it might keep me awake, and I sure didn't want to go back to sleep with that dream waiting for me.

Later, Pastor Mac came. I finally had a chance to explain to someone how all this happened and that I didn't do nothing to deserve being in this trouble.

"Remember that day in the store when you grabbed Johnny Smallhead, and there was the man with the crutches, and next to him was a man with a mustache?"

"Aye, that'd be Wilkes," he pulled at his beard. "He's a strange one. Don't know much about him, but he friendlied up to Melvin and them two were always together."

"Yeah, well I'm sure he's the one who killed Melvin and that's his whiskey-makin' stuff out there. I saw them go into the woods, then the other one, Wilkes, came hurryin' out and ran off."

Mac listened, then said, "I'll tell the sheriff that. But you got another problem, Dorky."

"Man, I don't need no more problems!"

"Aye, well, they got a warrant from the judge to search the *Killdeer* and they found some bottles of illegal whiskey hidden in your engine room."

I felt like I was going to throw-up "That 'Wilkes' fella musta put them there last night!"

"I'm sure that's the case. Problem is, how do we convince the sheriff of that?"

Pastor Mac prayed with me and handed me a Bible through the bars. "This here will give you faith and hope. In the meantime, I've called our attorney, Bradley, and he'll be coming to talk to you. Keep praying, boy, and you'll be okay." He left.

I flipped the Bible open and read the first verse that caught my eye:

> *Do not be overcome by evil,*
> *but overcome evil with good.*
> *Romans 12:20-21*

The only 'good' I knew how to do was pray. I prayed that Jason's mother would get well and that Jason would be well and happy. I prayed for Johnny and Pete finding work that they'd like. I prayed for Wil—asked that he be successful in his school to be a pastor. I prayed for everyone I knew and asked God to bless them all. I prayed that Wilkes would be found and I'd be proven innocent of all the bad things the sheriff was charging me with. Finally, I prayed for Sheriff Sardino. I asked God to open the sheriff's eyes to see that I wasn't guilty.

The door clanked open. "Okay, son." The sheriff unlocked the cell and led me to the office. "Someone here to see you."

Attorney Bradley shook my hand. "Dor, I'm sorry you've been caught up in this mess," he motioned me to a chair. "We'll get it straightened out. I'm not a criminal attorney, but I can ensure that you are represented up to the time of a trial—if it comes to that."

"He wasn't 'caught up,'" said the sheriff. "He was just plain 'caught.'" He laughed at what he thought was a joke.

"Is there someplace where we can be alone, sheriff?" said Bradley.

"Y'all just sit here and have your little talk. I'm goin' be gone for a bit." The sheriff got up, hoisted his pants up over his belly, and went out, slamming the door.

I told Bradley the whole story. He took notes on a little pad, nodding from time to time, making grunting sounds. He told me to tell Sheriff Sardino exactly what I told him, and only that. He'd be there with me, he said.

The sheriff came back, "You ready to make your confession, boy?"

"I ain't goin' to confess nothin," I said. "Cause I ain't done nothin' to confess to."

"Yup, that's what they all say." He sat behind the desk and took up a pencil and paper.

"What are the charges against my client?" asked Bradley.

"Suspicion of murder, operating an illegal still, withholding evidence and resisting arrest."

"I didn't 'resist arrest' and you know it!"

"There, you see," said the sheriff. "He's doin' it again. This boy just don't cooperate with the investigation."

"The murdered man, sheriff," said Bradley. "What was his name?"

"Well, first off, we have a dead riverboat owner, Capt. Johnathan Hannah. Died under mysterious circumstances, and now a man named Melvin Mulder was found beaten to death with this here boy standin' over him with the murder weapon in his hand, the dead man's own crutch. And we found illegal whiskey hidden aboard his boat." He lit a cigar and scratched at the back of his head. "On top of all that, we're investigating the willful destruction of the Quickville pier by your client while piloting the dead Captain's boat. I don't know, Mr. Bradley, but this ain't lookin' too good for this here client of your's."

Mr. Bradley finished taking notes. "At what have you set bail?"

The sheriff snickered, "There ain't no 'bail' for this man. Bootleggin' is a federal matter, and I have to keep him right here for the feds."

"Just take it easy, Dor," said Bradley. "Is there anything I can bring you?"

"I'd surely like a pillow and blanket off the boat, sir, if you wouldn't mind."

As the gray light coming through the window bars grew more faint, Pastor Mac brought me a blanket and pillow. "I found out from Mason Quick that the Quickville pier had been condemned more than two years ago, Dorky." He smiled. "At least that's one less thing they can charge you with."

"Did you find Wilkes?"

"He's not at his usual hangouts, and his apartment still has all of his things there, so I don't think he fled." He pulled at his beard like he did when thinking. "I'm goin' over to Nussome. I've heard him talk about some kinfolk he has over there."

Nussome was a small town about five miles east of Quickville.

After Pastor Mac left, I held the Bible close, pulled the blanket up over my head and tried to bury myself in the pillow. "Thank you Lord for Pastor Mac and Mr. Bradley. Please help them, and show the sheriff that I'm not the killer. Please help Mac and Mr. Bradley find Mr. Wilkes and some proof that I didn't do anything wrong." I looked for my light, but there was only the blackness in my vision. "Lord, remember when Your light was still with me, even after I'd ignored it. Thank You Father, and I'll do my best to do as Your word says, *I won't be overcome by evil, and I'll overcome evil with goodness.* Please help me, Lord." There was still no light.

I prayed for everyone again—even myself. I slept better that night, without the scary dreams.

In the morning, two federal agents came to the jail. I heard them talk to the sheriff in loud voices. They came back to where I was. The oldest one asked me a lot of questions. The other stood to the side and shook his head and looked at the sheriff sometimes like he was still angry. When they left, I heard the older one say, "You ever hear of *evidence*, sheriff? You have no *evidence*!" In a couple of minutes, the front door slammed.

Later that morning, Attorney Bradley told me that the sheriff had no proof that I had anything to do with the whiskey making. Also the pier had been condemned and the sheriff had neglected to post signs on it, so I might have a lawsuit against the City of Quickville for damage done to *Killdeer* when the pier came apart.

"I don't want to sue anybody, Mr. Bradley," I said. "I just want to get out of here and get back to work on my riverboat."

"I think we'll have you out of here soon, Dor. The sheriff has no witnesses, no solid evidence at all. You have no motive, and he'll look foolish if he takes this into a court of law."

"We gotta find that Wilkes fella," I said.

"Pastor Mac and I are on that. Also, some of the townspeople are watching Wilkes' place and your boat." He smiled. "Cheer up, son, If he shows up, we'll know it."

I folded the blankets and straightened the pillows. I rolled up the mattress on the end of the bed so it would air out, and put the pillows and blankets on top of it like I once saw in a movie about the Army. The door opened and Sheriff Sardino came in carrying a plate and a plastic cup. The plate was covered with a napkin and the cup had a plastic top on it. I knew it was my lunch from the diner in town.

"You sure like to keep things neat, don't you boy?" He slipped the food through the slot.

"Yessir," I said. "Capt. Hannah said that a tidy ship is a happy ship, and one of my jobs on *Killdeer* was to keep things straight. He didn't want no messes anyplace."

"You didn't like him much, did you?"

That surprised me. "Oh, no sir, you're wrong there." I went to the bars and he stepped back like he thought I was going to do something to him. "Capt. Hannah was about the best friend I ever had—except for Pastor Mac. He taught me how to be a river boatman, and even willed his boat to me."

"So that's why you killed him, hmm?" he looked serious. "To get the boat?"

"No, sheriff. He had something bad wrong with him all along. He didn't tell me what it was. That's what killed him. I could never hurt the captain." I went back and sat on the bare bed springs.

"MacAndrew tells me that you lived with him when his church was destroyed." He pointed a fat finger at me. "You have anything to do with that?"

I could see the sheriff was trying to find something more to charge me with. "No, I'd never do anything to make Pastor Mac unhappy, and that made him terrible unhappy."

"Wait, you're the boy that MacAndrew saved when the levee broke through, right?"

I said, "Yes, I'm that boy."

"I remember the newspaper story. You ran away after that, right?"

"Yes I left."

He kept looking for more. "Why'd you leave?"

"I asked my light if Pastor Mac could get a new, large church. It said yes, then the old church fell apart so he had to get a new church," I was talking too fast and thinking of how I felt then. "I was just causin' Pastor Mac trouble, so I left, and then I woke up on the riverboat. That's how I met Capt. Hannah."

"You asked your *what*?" He was looking at me funny. I realized then that I told him about my light. Now he'd think I was really a crazy man.

"I asked God to come into my life," I explained slowly. "Pastor Mac helped me do that, and then I saw this light when I closed my eyes at night. My light would blink when it answered yes to my question or prayer."

The sheriff looked down at the floor for a long time, then said, "It made things happen for you, did it?"

"Yes sir, it did. But it's gone now." I waited for him to make fun of me.

"Well," he pointed his finger at me again. "I'm going to give this 'light' of yours a little test. I have a daughter who is really sick, and the doctors don't know what's wrong with her. You ask this 'light' of yours to make her well." He headed for the door.

I called after him, "The light is gone, Sheriff, but I'll pray real hard for her. What's her name?"

"Kate's her name. 'Katie' we call her."

That night I closed my eyes and my light was not there. I prayed, "Dear God, I know that *You* are the light and the light that is in me is You, the Father, Jesus, the Son, and the Holy Spirit, and you can do all things. You say in the Bible, 'You have not because you ask not,' so I'm asking that you touch Sheriff Sardino's daughter, Kate, and heal her of her illness, dear Lord."

I prayed harder than I ever had before. I felt bad for the sheriff and for his daughter, and I cried as I prayed for her.

I couldn't go to sleep. I got up and walked back and forth in the tiny cell, still praying and asking God for some sort of sign that my prayers were being heard. I guess I expected too much too soon. I remembered that Pastor Mac said that God does what He does when He wants to do it, and that we don't understand His ways.

I picked up my Bible and knelt next to the bunk, "Dear Lord, I guess I don't know Your ways, but I do know that Your way is the right way, so I guess I'll just let You handle things . . ." I guess that's what God wanted to hear, because I fell asleep before I finished my prayer, kneeling at the side of the jail bed my hands still clutching my Bible.

Chapter Thirteen

**"Test me in this," says the
LORD Almighty, "and see if
I will not throw open the
floodgates of heaven and pour
out so much blessing that
there will not be room enough
to store it."**

Malachi 3:10

"Pastor Mac came to see you last night," said Sheriff Sardino. He opened the cell door and brought in breakfast. "But you were sleepin' like a dead man on the floor. He put the mattress down for you, covered you up. We had a long talk."

I wondered what they talked about, but I had my mouth full of pancakes and couldn't ask.

"We talked mostly about you," he went on. "I guess you've had a rough time of it. Not that it excuses anything you've done, but Katie is about your age, and she's having a rough time too, so I can sort of sympathize with your situation. Not that I condone any of what you've done . . ."

"Sheriff, I ain't done anythin' like what you think I . . ."

"Don't interrupt me boy!" He sounded just like Capt. Hannah. "What I'm tryin' to get around to sayin' is that I might have been a little too aggressive chargin' you with Capt. Hannah's death, and bootleggin'—you ain't been around here enough to have been operatin' that still. And destroyin' the city dock, well, that old pile of lumber has been ready to fall into the river for years."

I stopped eating, and said, "That leaves the killin' of Mr. Mulder still on me, but honest, sheriff, I never even talked to him, or Mr. Wilkes either."

Sheriff Sardino said quietly, "Pastor Mac is going back to Nussome today looking for Wilkes. You talk to your light about Katie?"

"No. I told you before that I don't have the light any more. But I prayed really hard for her last night. I think God will touch her."

"When?"

"*When*? I don't know when. I guess it'll be when God decides it's time. Maybe Pastor Mac has some idea how God works. I got no idea. Why don't you talk to him about it? He's a lot smarter than I am about how God works."

Sheriff Sardino seemed angry, like I should be able to give him a better answer. He grabbed my tray and cup and slammed the door behind him.

I just sat through the next day. Nobody came to talk to me. The deputy brought my meals. He didn't talk much. I was getting lonely and more worried about how I'd ever get out of this mess. I continued to pray in the mornings, many times during the long day, and for hours into the evening. I didn't pray for myself. I prayed that Pastor Mac would be safe and well, and that he'd find Mr. Wilkes. I prayed for Wil, the sheriff, but mostly for Katie. I felt that I was able to heal her through Jesus and through my prayers. I guess I was testing that idea.

I read in the Bible that Jesus asked to be tested;

"Test me in this," says the
LORD Almighty, "and see if
I will not throw open the
floodgates of heaven and pour
out so much blessing that
there will not be room enough
to store it."
Malachi 3: 10

There was so much that I didn't know. I thought of Wil. When he came home from college, he'd be able to answer my questions just like Pastor Mac.

I think it was Friday when Mason Quick came to see me. He brought a chair from the sheriff's office and sat close to the bars, pad and pencil in hand. "This is the first time Sheriff Sardino has let me see you, Dor," he said. "Please tell me your side of what happened out there at the still."

I told him the whole story. He was writing like crazy, poking his tongue with the pencil like he did the first time I met him. I keep forgetting to ask Pastor Mac why he did that.

"And that's it, Mr. Quick," I finished. Then I asked him what the folks in town were saying.

"Everyone thinks you're absolutely innocent, Dor, including me," he said as he put his pencil behind his ear. "Seems like Sheriff Sardino is the only one who thinks you're guilty of wrongdoing."

The door burst open. "Mr. Quick," the deputy was almost yelling. "Sheriff just got a call from the Preacher. He found Wilkes in Nussome, and the sheriff just left to go get them."

Mr. Quick rushed out the door, dragging the chair. "I'll be back to see you, Dor," he called over his shoulder.

I lay down to read the Bible, but fell asleep. A ruckus in the sheriff's office woke me. I could hear the sheriff's voice and a lot of mumbling. Then the door flew open and Wilkes was led in, staggering and bumping into the walls. He was very drunk and the deputy staggered with him into the cell across from mine.

Pastor Mac said, "Well, my young friend, we found our suspect, and I suspect you'll be out of here soon." He came closer and lowered his voice, "I had quite a talk with our sheriff, lad. He is very concerned about his daughter, Katie, I think's her name, and said that you're prayin' hard for her. God bless you, boy. Sheriff Sardino will be comin' to church on Sunday, thanks to you."

The sheriff came up. "When this drunken fool sobers up, we'll see what he has to say." Wilkes was snoring loudly. "Meantime, I'm going to release you into Pastor Mac's custody. You'll not leave town, fella, or I'll have you back here and locked-up tighter than a girdle on a 'gator, Got that?"

"Yes sir, sheriff, I got that for sure!" He opened the cell and Mac threw his arm around my shoulders and we walked out into the daylight. What a wonderful feeling to be free!

"I want to see you tomorrow afternoon, Dor," said Sheriff Sardino.

I wanted to go to *Killdeer* and see that she was okay, but Pastor Mac said that as long as I was in his custody I'd better stay with him and Mrs. MacAndrew. After a big meal, we spent the evening talking, then we prayed. I went to bed in Wil's room. It felt so good to be out of that old jailhouse, and I told God that. My light was not there, but I knew that God was.

Pastor Mac worked on his sermons while I worked on *Killdeer*. I helped him at the church. We worked together preparing me for my test. Time went by fast. Two weeks later, all charges against me were dropped as Wilkes tearfully confessed to hitting Melvin Mulder with the crutch in what he said was self-defense.

I was dusting and straightening up the Bibles and hymnals, getting ready for Sunday service when Sheriff Sardino came in. "Dor," he said, quietly, I guess because he was in the church, "I gotta talk to you."

"Sure, sheriff." I followed him outside and he stopped at a car, leaning his arm on the top. Someone was inside.

"This here's my daughter, Katie," he tilted his head toward the car. She was small and pale and as skinny as a river reed, but her beautiful smile glowed, brightening her face.

"We came to thank you, son, for your prayers and for carin' about little Katie here."

I found it hard to say anything. "Well, uh . . . I didn't do nothin' really . . ."

"You have," he insisted. "My Katie has been improvin' some every day since you and Pastor Mac—and me—been prayin' for her. It's a miracle, boy, and you got it goin' for us."

Katie leaned forward and reached out to me. I took her bony little hand, afraid of breaking her tiny fingers. "Thank you, Dor," she said. Her voice was as small as she.

"Will you sit with us in church this mornin'?" Sheriff Sardino wasn't the same mean, gruff, loud man I'd known. He had softened up, I guess because Katie was there.

"Sure, Sheriff," I said.

I met them at the door just before the service started. "Lead the way," said the sheriff. We sat where I usually do, Katie between the sheriff and me. People mumbled to each other and smiled and some spoke to Katie, saying how good it was to be seeing her there. When Pastor Mac prayed, Katie held my hand and bowed her little head.

With all of the charges dropped, Pastor Mac drove me up to Barriston to re-take the Riverboat Master's exam. I had been studying most all the time for the past three months and felt that this time there would be no problem passing it. Pastor Mac visited with Attorney Bradley while I spent three hours at the test center. It was almost the same test. This time I really knew the answers and realized that when I took it the first time, I wasn't ready. I just thought I was.

I felt good about how the test went and joined Mac and Mr. Bradley at the attorney's office. Mr. Bradley said that recently he had to tell some customers that *Killdeer* wasn't able to carry their freight. He was afraid that we'd lost some of them. Some would wait. When *Killdeer* was back to work, we'd have some catching-up to do. That was good news. Now I needed to find a stoker and a crew.

While in Barriston, we went into a corner drugstore and Mac bought a safety razor and shaving soap. "You gonna shave off your beard?" I asked him.

"No, lad, you're going to shave off those wee whiskers that have been pokin' themselves out of your chin!"

I looked in a mirror and sure enough, there were little whiskers I'd never noticed before.

"Seems to me, boy, that you're growin' up," he said.

For the next month I helped Pastor Mac with some work at his house, and at the church cleaning and repairing things. I ached to get back to running *Killdeer* and back on the river. If you know and love the river, you learn that it not only flows toward the Gulf, it also courses through your veins. It flows through your heart, and floods your mind. It's always with you like an incurable virus that infects you with a deep love for that old, brown, frothing mass of snags and currents.

It was a rainy October morning when Pastor Mac came knocking on *Killdeer*. "Dorky! Dorky!" he called.

I came up out of the engine room where I was shifting the coal so that it wouldn't get hot. It could start to fire if left piled up and damp.

"Hi, Pastor Mac," I said. "You're out early this gloomy mornin'."

"Aye, that I am, me lad." He looked cold and tired. "Would ye be comin' up to our house this evenin' for some dinner?"

"For some of Mrs. MacAndrew's cookin'? You bet!"

The rest of that day I worked with energy, knowing that I'd have a wonderful dinner with those I love.

I cleaned up as best I could and walked up to the MacAndrew house just as it was getting dark. It was brightly lit inside. There were a couple of cars parked in the driveway. One was Sheriff Sardino's.

Reaching the porch, I could hear happy talking and laughing and wondered if maybe Pastor Mac had made a mistake. Maybe this was a party. I was never invited to parties. Mrs. MacAndrew let me in. The sheriff, and Mac, and Mason Quick, all shook my hand and said how good it was to see me. I thought that was strange since they'd all seen me just hours or days before.

Katie Sardino was there, looking like she was not so sick and frail. She came over to me and gave me a hug. No girl ever hugged me before.

"I'm very glad you came, Dorky," she said.

"Uh, me too," I stammered.

I said hello to everyone and Mrs. MacAndrew called us to the table. She showed me that I was to sit at the end of the table, the small end where there was only one chair, and Pastor Mac sat at the other end. We looked at each other down the length of it. I think it was called a "place of honor," but I didn't know why they would be honoring me.

Katie was at my right, Mr. Quick at my left, and Mrs. Mac sat at the right hand of Pastor Mac.

"My dear Mr. Walker," said Mac when everyone had quieted. "Would you please honor us with the blessing."

I had never said Grace with people other than Pastor and Mrs. Mac and Wil around, and I was nervous. I started, "Dear Lord, we thank you . . . we come to this here table, Lord . . ." I was lost and glanced up at Mac. He smiled and winked at me, like I was doing fine. "We come to this table Lord with thanks for this wonderful food, and all the blessings we enjoy through Your grace and love. Uh . . . We thank you for this time spent with our dear friends and ask that you continue to bless them, this house and this family. Lead us and direct us. We pray this in your son, Jesus' Holy name, Amen."

"Amen," said the people. Katie touched my arm and said, "You should be a preacher, Dor, that was good." Sheriff Sardino handed me a bowl of mashed potatoes, and grunted, "Yeah, good."

The food was so tasty that I ate until I thought my belt would break. Then, while we were having coffee, Mrs. MacAndrew came out of the kitchen carrying a big cake with a lot of candles burning and smoking on top of it.

I leaned over and asked Katie, "Whose havin' a birthday?"

"You, silly!" Her face aglow, she laughed.

Pastor Mac stood, "Folks, this young friend of ours, Dorky Walker, has reached a milestone of life. On this day, 21-years ago he came into this world, and on this day five years ago he came into our lives. A wet, dirty, lonesome orphan, he has worked hard and learned so very much. We're proud of you, Dorky. Happy birthday!"

I knew that people had birthdays, but I never thought that I'd be one of them, since I didn't know when I was born. Nobody ever told me that I could have a birthday party too. I asked Mac about that.

"I snooped around, looked at county records and found that you were born in Kennsington, Miss. on October 20th." He handed me a piece of paper. It was my birth certificate from Kennsington. Sure enough, it said *Dorky Walker.*

"We had to have it for you to be able to take the riverboat exam." He smiled. "I kept it quiet until we could have a proper birthday party for you."

The party went until late that night, and everyone was real nice to me. It was about the best time I'd ever had. Me and Katie talked a lot. She was very smart and said a lot of funny things. I don't think I'd ever laughed so much in one night before. And she always held on to my arm or hand. I liked that.

"You're the first boy my daddy ever liked," she said. I liked that, even though the Sheriff never much showed it.

"Well, you're the first girl that ever showed me any mind." She squeezed my hand with a lot more strength than I'd ever expected. I guess she really was getting better.

She kissed me on the cheek when she and the sheriff left that night.

Since all the charges against me were dropped, I was staying on the *Killdeer* again. It was early on a Friday morning when Pastor Mac knocked on the side of the cabin. "Hey there, Capt. Walker, are ye aboard this here vessel, lad? I've a letter for ye."

Rubbing my eyes and yawning, I read;

"Dear Mr. Dorky Walker,

Congratulations, I am pleased to inform you that your score on the Riverboat Master's examination met our standards for the Captaincy for which you applied. Your score total of 97 percent is more than needed for successful completion of the examination. The Certificate is enclosed herein and is valid for a period of five (5) years from its date of origin.

    Contact the River Authority with any questions.

Albert Fitzsimmons,

Administrator, River Authority"

Chapter Fourteen

**"You have persevered and
have endured hardships
for my name, and have
not grown weary."
Revelation 2:2-4**

The rest of October and November was cold, gloomy and rainy, and the river ran fast and dirty, filled to her banks from rains and snow up north.

Wil would be coming home for Christmas break, and if I could find a stoker to work a few days, we could make a couple of river runs. That would depend a lot on the river. It would have to run lower, calm-down, and slow-down. I spent a lot of time praying for those things.

In the middle of November, I got a letter from Jason's mother.

Dear Mr. Walker,

Jason has been telling me how good you treat him and how he likes to work with you on that boat. He come home to tend to me, but I am all better now and he wants to know if you need him to work again.

Jessy Jones—Jason's mama.

I jumped up and down and ran to the old desk to write her back. My prayers were being answered awfully fast!

Two weeks later, Jason was on board, Wil was home and eager to make a river run in *Killdeer*, and the river's level had dropped, steadying to a calm flow. Attorney Bradley had three loads arranged for us. All we needed was a deck crew and we could get to work.

"Why you need a deck crew, Mr. Walker?" asked Jason. "The three of us, you, Mr. Wil, and me, why, we can load as good as anybody."

"I don't know, Jason. When will we get any rest?"

He smiled that big smile, "We can take turns sleepin'. You know how to stoke them furnaces. Mr. Wil and me can steer the boat. What ya think?"

We left for Barriston that night. The river was smooth with just enough moonlight to see by. While Wil steered, I planned our trip schedule. Barriston to Lewisport, then back downriver to Barriston where we'd load up and make three stops on the way back to Quickville. We'd be gone six days with one day somewhere between Barriston and Quickville on Sunday. We'd not run on Sunday, and find a church wherever we were.

It was good to be back on the river, feeling the boat vibrating and shaking under my feet. The familiar sounds of the engine and the big old paddlewheel slapping at the water, pushing us along. Not fast, but steady and true. I took the helm and Wil took a nap.

The river was mysterious at night. Dark things flew over and around the boat and sometimes big, shiny shapes splashed into the water from the shore. Mostly bats and alligators spooked by our passing, I supposed. Large riverboats, all lit up like a city with music and folks wandering around their decks, gave us answering whistle blasts as we approached. Most all the people waved as we passed. Then it would be dark and quiet again except for the steady "thunk-a, thunk-a, thunk-a," of the engine and the "squeak, squeak, squeak," of the lantern swinging overhead.

We took turns at the wheel, but I had trouble sleeping when Jason or Wil were at the helm. I guess Capt. Hannah must have been just as nervous when I was doing it all alone.

We docked at Barriston, and the loading was easy, mainly because Jason was so strong. He shoved things around like a tractor. Wil and I mostly just steered them into the boat. I decided that Jason should get double pay, his regular wage, plus a deck hand's salary as well.

At Lewiston, we delivered the cargo and picked up a small load to take back to Barriston. We had to stop at the coal dock, then headed downstream from there.

We were enjoying everything, the river run, the stops along the way, even the hard work of loading and unloading.

We were able to pick up a big load in Barriston that was headed for Quickville, thanks to Attorney Bradley's hard work. I visited his office and he gave me the newest figures on *Killdeer's* account. There was still some money, but it had gone fast since I hadn't been able to work the boat.

We pulled out into the river's current on a Saturday, headed for Quickville. We'd need to stop along the way and find a church to go to on Sunday, and it looked like it might be in Duvalle, a small town on the river that had an ample dock.

We tied up late Saturday night and went into town to eat and find the church. The lady at the restaurant said their Pastor was in the hospital in Barriston, and that there would be no church service that Sunday.

Wil said, "Dor, look, we can have a service on the back deck of *Killdeer*! I've done sermons before at school, and I can use the practice, and give the town's folk their church service! What do you think?"

"Sure, Wil, but how can we get the people to come?" I didn't think we would get many people on such a short notice. The restaurant lady got on the telephone, and the next morning we had the back deck filled with townspeople, all dressed in their best. Wil's sermon was good. He didn't look nervous and the little congregation seemed happy. We took a collection and gave it to the mayor to give to the pastor of their church. Many, especially the men, hung around talking about the boat and the river, and the runs we make. Best of all, the lady from the restaurant invited us to dinner that night.

Back on the river Monday morning, we made good time to Quickville. The river was running fast, but not so fast that there were a lot of things afloat to dodge. We docked at the slough in Quickville just as the sun was sliding down behind the river's treeline.

Mason Quick hurried to the dock as we were tying up. "Wil, Dor, Pastor MacAndrew is very ill. You boys should get right on over there. He's at home. The doctor's with him!"

We shut down everything and ran to the MacAndrew house. Mac was in bed, looking sort of gray. The doctor said not to be long.

"Pastor Mac," I whispered. "It's Dorky and Wil. Are you all right?" As soon as I said that I realized what a stupid question it was. Of course he wasn't "all right." He was really sick.

He opened his eyes, but seemed to have trouble focusing. "Ah, me lads," he whispered. "How'd the trip go?"

"Ah . . . great Mac. We didn't have any problems, and had a church service onboard in Duvalle."

His eyes brightened and he smiled a little. "Did my boy, Wil, give the sermon?"

"I sure did Pastor Mac," said Wil. "And they invited us back too."

"Ah, I've been blessed with two fine lads. I'm very proud of both of you, y'know."

He reached out and gripped my hand. "Dorky, do you still have your light?"

"No sir, not for a long time now, and I don't know why."

"Aye, I suspected as much, boy." His whisper was weaker and I had to lean down to hear him. "Get my Bible, lad, and look to Hebrews 5:14, will ya."

I quickly leafed through the pages of the Bible to Hebrews, Chapter 5, and found Verse 14, and read out loud:

> *Anyone who lives on milk, being*
> *still an infant, is not acquainted*
> *with the teaching about righteousness.*
> *But solid food is for the mature,*
> *who by constant use have trained*
> *themselves to distinguish*
> *good from evil.*
> *Hebrews 5: 14*

I sure didn't understand that right away, then Mac said that "milk" would be my light. I had outgrown that which it offered: "teaching of righteousness." So now I had "solid food" and must use my "maturity" to know right from wrong. I didn't *need* my light any more!

"The Holy Spirit is still with you, lad," said Mac. "Always will be. Your light is still in you as well. You've outgrown the need for it on a day-to-day basis. It may, or may not, return sometime—only God knows which it'll be."

"Wil, my boy," he said. "Will you lead my flock at Kirkcaldy Christian Church until I recover from this?"

I looked at Wil and he had tears running down his cheeks. He said in a small, squeaky voice, "Sure Mac, I'll do my best 'til you come back."

The doctor came in, "Boys," he said, "you best go now and let Pastor Mac get some rest."

I left Wil there and walked to *Killdeer*. I felt like I was going to cry, but if I did, that would mean Mac was really bad sick. I didn't want that.

Jason had the boat all settled-in and was snoring softly down in the engine room. I went up the wheelhouse. I hadn't completed the log book entries for our trip. Capt. Hannah's stub of a pencil was sticking out of the log at the page for that day. I opened the book and held the pencil, thinking of that Bible verse: *"Solid food is for the mature."* It told me that I am old enough now to begin figuring things out for myself. I touched the end of the pencil to my tongue and entered the time we had docked. Being damp, the pencil slid easily and smoothly across the paper and left darker, easier to read numbers. "Ah, now I see why Mason Quick licks his pencil!" I thought. I could imagine what Capt. Hannah would say, "Well it sure took you long enough to figure that out, you hollow-headed lump of marsh mud!" And I guess Pastor Mac would say something like, "Aye, me boy, you sure enough figured that out, you did!" I said a prayer for the captain and for the pastor.

I slept an uneasy sleep. Sometime during the night I was back in the bottom of the round room, and the hairy black spider sat on the spring above me. It began to bounce, bounce, bounce, each time getting closer and closer to me. But this time I wasn't so much frightened as I was angry.

"I don't have time for your stupid games, spider," I said. I remembered that Jesus told Satan in Matthew 4, "Away from me,

Satan!" Really mad now, I yelled, "In the name of the Father, Son, and Holy Spirit, get away from me, spider! I'm not a kid any more!"

The spider stopped its advance, shuddered, and began to fall apart. Black hair, pieces of its body and legs crumbled into small pieces and were carried out the top of the round room like dirty, black smoke up a chimney. The spring dissolved into nothingness, as did my anger. I thanked God for ridding me of that pest. I had finally outgrown that nightmare of fear.

A tapping on the hull woke me. Duke Farley, the boatyard owner, stood on the dock, looking serious. "I just got a call from Mrs. MacAndrew," he said nervously. "Pastor Mac has gone to be with the Lord. He passed away quietly last night sometime. I'm sorry boy."

I muttered, "Thanks, Mr. Farley," and went to the wheelhouse. I sat on the old stool that Capt. Hannah had just about worn out, and cried.

"Dear Lord," I prayed. "Please take Pastor Mac into your arms and give him a place of honor in Heaven. Y'know, God, I never had a real father. Capt. Hannah was almost a father to me, and Pastor Mac was about as good a father any boy could have, I guess." I stopped crying and felt a little anger growing in my chest.

"I don't get it, Lord. You gave me Pastor Mac. You gave me Capt. Hannah. You gave me my light. Now, Lord, you've taken them all away. What's the point of all this?"

I went back down to the bunk and lay in the darkness. "And Dear God, help me to understand why I can't have a real father like other boys."

Mason Quick reported that Pastor Mac's funeral was the biggest event in a half century in Quickville, only surpassed by those of the Quick family. Wil led the service and did a good job. Katie was there with her father and she looked a lot better—stronger and happier. She sat up front with Wil and Mrs. MacAndrew. There was a reception at the MacAndrew place after, but I didn't go. I just couldn't be around the families when I was all alone now.

Back at *Killdeer*, Pete was sitting on the dock. "Hey, Captain," he said, "I'm sure sorry to hear about Pastor Mac."

"Yeah, thanks, Pete. Whadda doin' here?"

"Well," he looked down at the splintered planks of the old pier, "old Johnny got himself put in the N'orlin's jail, and I figered I'd better get gone of that place, so I came here."

He looked tired and dirty. "The law after you?" I asked.

"Naw, I got out of there before they knew anything about me."

"Okay, Pete, same job, same pay, but you'll have to clean yourself up. You got any money?"

Pete had a few dollars, so I gave him a few more so that he could go into town and get a room, a bath and something to eat. "Be here at 6 in the morning, okay?"

"I'll be here. Thanks, Captain!" He hurried down the dock, whistling.

We had a load to pick up downstream of Quickville, a place called Lancerton. I'd never been there. That part of the river was strange to me. I went slowly and carefully. It was only about 12 miles, so we were there before noon. Lancerton had a long dock with what looked like a warehouse at one end. I pulled *Killdeer* up there and Pete tied her up.

The place looked familiar to me. After arranging for the cargo to be loaded, I walked into the little town. It was the town where that lady, what was her name? Louise! She fed me then drugged me. I found the little restaurant and went into the side door.

Louise looked up at me as I came in. "This here's the kitchen, fella, you gotta go 'round front to eat."

Naw, Louise," I said, "I ate here once before and got a bad headache."

She recognized me then and backed away from the stove, looking around for some sort of weapon. "Oh, it's you," she muttered, "the boy with the funny name. Whadda ya want?"

She was scared. I reached into my back pant's pocket. She stiffened and backed farther away. I took a $5 bill out of my wallet and dropped it on the table. "I thank you for feedin' me when I was here last, and thank you for meeting me up with Capt. Hannah on the riverboat *Killdeer*."

She was shaking with fear, eyes the size of the pots on the stove. "I didn't mean you no harm, boy," she stammered. "It was all Skerv's idea, him and the captain."

I smiled, turned, and left. I can imagine the relief she must have felt, and I figured it'd be a long, long time before she drugged another boy.

We made four more runs up and down that old river that month, never once getting into Quickville. I went to church in Duvalle the last Sunday and met up with the Donnovan's. They were farmers outside of town and had a daughter, Mary Sue.

I really liked Katie, but I really liked Mary Sue Donnovan, too. Maybe more. I decided that I'd have to make more trips to Duvalle.

Finally, back in Quickville in the middle of September, I gave *Killdeer's* whistle three long blasts as we pulled into the slough. By the time we got tied to the dock, the old pier was full of townsfolk.

"Your timing is perfect!" It was Wil, standing with Katie. They both looked great.

"What 'timing' is that, Wil?" I asked.

They came aboard, both hugged me long and strong.

"Well," said Katie, "tomorrow's Wil's birthday, and to celebrate that, Wil and I are getting married. We want you to be our best man!"

I was stunned. I was happy. I was sad. I was glad that I'd met Mary Sue too, now that Katie was marrying Wil. I wished Mary Sue could be there for the wedding.

We all went to the church where a dinner was all prepared and Wil and Katie's wedding was announced. Sheriff Sardino was there, all dressed-up and looking proud. He shook my hand and threw his big arm around my shoulders. "I thought you might be Katie's husband some day, Dorky," he said, "but your friend and our preacher, Wil, will make Katie a mighty fine husband." He looked at me serious like and sort of whispered, "You okay?"

"Sure, Sheriff." I told him about Mary Sue in Duvalle and said that I sure wish she could be there.

The next morning, I dressed in my best clothes and walked to the church. Wil hustled me into a back room and handed me a hanger with a black suit. "Put this on!" He was nervous.

It was a tuxedo. I'd never worn a tuxedo before and had some trouble figuring out the little funny tie and the belly strap. I finished dressing and went outside to get some air.

"Capt. Walker!" I wasn't used to being called "Captain" and didn't realize the call was for me until it was repeated. I turned and saw Mr. and Mrs. Donnovan and Mary Sue happily waving.

"How'd y'all know about this?" I asked.

"Well," said Mr. Donnovan, "your sheriff called us last night and drove up to Duvalle and picked us up this morning. It's his daughter gettin' hitched, and also Pastor Wil's birthday. We couldn't miss that."

At the altar, I felt a mite silly standing up there in that tuxedo with nothing to do but hand over the ring to Wil. It went well, and I don't guess I ever saw two happier people.

Mary Sue held my hand all during the party after the ceremony. It was a double party, with everyone wishing the bride and groom good things, and Wil a happy birthday.

That evening, Sheriff Sardino drove us all to Duvalle. The Donnovans shook my hand a wished me a happy birthday again. Mary Sue kissed me goodbye. I felt really good that night.

"Thanks for bringin' those folks to the weddin', Sheriff," I said as we headed back to Quickville.

"No thanks necessary, Dorky. I've been wanting to do something for you. I treated you pretty roughly at the jail. Your prayers healed my Katie." We were quiet the rest of the way to the *Killdeer's* dock, but for the first time ever, I began to think about having a car of my own. Only problem was, I didn't know how to drive.

The next day Pete, Jason, and I got an early start for a run up to Lewisport. It would be a long, slow, upstream trip. We'd probably get there early the next morning to pick up a heavy load of tractor parts going to Duvalle. I was excited thinking that I might be able to see Mary Sue Donnovan while in Duvalle, but mostly, my thoughts were of getting a car and learning to drive.

Killdeer seemed to be eager to get going. She sort of trembled at the dock, like a puppy ready to be taken for a walk. The old boat seemed to have developed a personality. We shoved off right on time, as Jason's singing rumbled up from the engine room, and echoed throughout the boat.

"Pete, you know how to drive a car?" I asked as he brought me a cup of coffee.

He laughed, "Sure. Everybody knows how to drive."

"I don't."

He looked at me like I was a two-headed frog. "You run this big old boat up and down the river, puttin' her into some of the dangdest, tightest docks and spaces I've ever seen, and you can't even drive a car?"

"Yup, that's about it." I felt a little foolish, but explained, "I ain't never had the chance to learn to drive, I've been so busy runnin' old *Killdeer* here."

"You need me to drive you someplace?" he asked.

"No." I said. "I really need you to teach me to drive. That is, as soon as I buy a car."

"You're going to buy a car without even bein' able to drive it?" He gave me the two-headed frog look again, but said that sure, he'd teach this old riverboatman how to drive a car.

We docked at Lewisport right on schedule, and we all got a chance to sleep for three hours before it was time to load the tractor parts aboard. I was so excited about the new challenge and opportunity to learn to drive, that once I was up, I left a note for Jason and Pete to do the loadin', and made my way into town at sunup.

I bought a newspaper from a little rack and sat on the curb, looking for cars for sale. Phew! There was a bunch of them! I went back to *Killdeer* and gave Pete the paper. I asked him to tell me which one of all the used cars would be the best for me. He selected a four door Oldsmobile, but I said it was too much money. We finally settled on a two door Ford, and when the loadin' was finished, I grabbed-up a bag of my money and we went into town, I bought it, and Pete drove it. From the passenger's seat, I watched everything he did. I practiced pushing the pedals and moving the shift lever like he was doing, all the way to the dock.

The Ford was loaded onto the bow deck of *Killdeer*, and we pulled out of Lewisport with a long, happy blast of our whistle.

We docked that evening at Duvalle and I ran to the Donnovan's house. Mary Sue was surprised to see me, but happy.

"I bought me a car so I can drive up here to see you," I exclaimed.

We went down to the dock and I showed her the Ford two door. "I'll come visitin' soon as I learn to drive it."

We talked for a while, then Mary Sue said, "I'll be right back—don't leave 'til I get back, okay?"

I helped with the last of the unloading and had just finished up when Mary Sue came running to the dock. "Daddy said that it's okay if I ride with you on your boat to Quickville tomorrow morning, if you'd let me!" She was out of breath and all red-faced.

"Sure," I said. "But how'll you get back home?"

Pete, standing nearby, said, "We'll drive her back in the Ford, and I can give you your first lesson." So it was settled. The Donnovans had us for dinner that night and I assured both of them that Mary Sue would be safe and well cared for on the river.

Mary Sue was standing at the boarding plank when I woke up the next morning, and we started on our way to Quickville. The river cooperated by being smooth and calm. *Killdeer* swept us downstream like a magic carpet. Pete at the helm, and Mary Sue and I held hands in the Ford as if we were driving it down the river.

Reflected sunbeams glistened across the water ahead of us, and cranes, egrets and ducks chattered as they swept overhead, flapping wildly in their haste to escape the imagined peril the old riverboat presented.

I heard the call of the Killdeer.

Mary Sue cuddled close and kissed me. I held her and felt a calm, happy bliss I had never experienced. We talked little, we just enjoyed being with each other as we cruised downriver in my Ford.

A short blast on the whistle told me that Pete was ready for me to take over the helm. I sure hated to leave Mary Sue.

At Quickville I docked *Killdeer* by nosing up to the boat yard's pier so that the car could be unloaded from the bow. Malcomb Farley was there and began the unloading without being told a thing. With the car on the dock, I moved the riverboat to the slough, secured everything, and asked Jason to watch over her while I drove Mary Sue back to Duvalle.

On the 20-mile drive to Duvalle, Pete showed me the basics of driving, the rules of the road, how to work the headlights, parking brake, horn, heater, and windshield wipers. I felt pretty confident that I could handle it.

Pete walked into town. I visited with the Donnovans, and said a late good night to Mary Sue. It was a couple of hours after sunset when I went to find Pete. In the first bar I came to I found him. Drunk. I got him back to the car and he fell into the back seat and was immediately asleep. I guessed that it was up to me to get us back to Quickville, and felt I could do it just fine. I started the car and the first thing I did was give it too much gas. It leaped forward, I braked hard. I heard a "thump" from the back seat. I stopped and saw that Pete had been tossed onto the floor. He didn't even wake up.

I eased it out onto the road and went four blocks before I remembered to turn on the headlights. The rest of the drive went well.

I enjoyed my very first driving experience and thought a lot about Mary Sue. I felt that someday, if she was willing, we might get married too, like Wil and Katie. I thought about how I'd come close to death a couple of times, how Pastor Mac saved me and helped me learn about the Bible and how he was about the best father a boy could ever have.

I remembered too Capt. Hannah and how he turned back to the Lord. Both of them are in heaven now, and that thought gave me peace.

It was funny how I was sent to the old riverboat, *Killdeer*, and it became my life. I'd learned a lot. Grew up. Have friends and a business that I really enjoy. God has been really good to me, and I guess I owe it all to Pastor MacAndrew.

I pulled into *Killdeer's* dock, covered Pete with his coat and left him on the back floor to sleep it off. I imagined that he'd slept in worse places. I walked to the water's edge and took a moment to thank God for all the blessings He had given me.

I heard the call of the Killdeer bird echo across the still water.

I felt good, happier than I could ever remember. I went aboard, quietly undressed, and slipped into my bunk. I gave another prayer of thanks to God for that day, for Mary Sue, and all my friends.

"Only thing else I need Lord, is someone to call dad like Katie, Mary Sue, and the rest of them have."

At that moment my light reappeared, shining brightly in the darkness. My heart was filled with joy. "Thank you, Dear God," I said aloud.

It was at then that I had a sensation that God was speaking to me, although I didn't hear a voice. It's hard to explain, but it was like I suddenly just *knew* what I was being told. It was as strong as if someone yelled into my ear, but I didn't actually hear anything.

The words were put into my heart and I'll never forget them:

"I am your Heavenly Father. You can call *Me* 'Dad.'"

And my light blinked off, and back on.

- END -